I0722383

The STEAL

Also from C. W. Gortner

The First Actress
The Romanov Empress
Marlene
The Vatican Princess
Mademoiselle Chanel
The Queen's Vow
The Confessions of Catherine De Medici
The Last Queen
The Tudor Secret
The Tudor Conspiracy
The Tudor Vendetta

Also from M.J. Rose

The Last Tiara
Cartier's Hope
Tiffany Blues
The Library of Light and Shadow
The Secret Language of Stones
The Witch of Painted Sorrows
The Collector of Dying Breaths
The Seduction of Victor H.
The Book of Lost Fragrances
The Hypnotist
The Memoirist
The Reincarnationist
Lip Service
In Fidelity
Flesh Tones
Sheet Music
The Halo Effect
The Delilah Complex
The Venus Fix
Lying in Bed

M.J. Rose and Steve Berry
The Museum of Mysteries
The Lake of Learning
The House of Long Ago
The End of Forever

M.J. Rose and C. W. Gortner
The Steal

The STEAL

C.W. GORTNER

and

M.J. ROSE

The Steal
By C. W. Gortner and M.J. Rose

Copyright 2021 C. W. Gortner and M.J. Rose
ISBN: 978-1-952457-54-8

Published by Blue Box Press, an imprint of Evil Eye Concepts, Incorporated

Chapter One

Jerome
1957

Everyone always says Cannes is one of the most beautiful places in the world. I guess they were right. It sure is beautiful today, the bright sunlight scattered across the Mediterranean, the elegant promenade shaded by palm trees like immense umbrellas, the fancy storefronts and cafés, the stylish restaurants and grand hotels forming a gilded ring against the rugged backdrop of southern France. Yeah, gorgeous. Picture-perfect, as they say. Like a movie set. No scars from the war here. Or, at least, none anyone can see.

And just like a movie set, it's the ideal setting for an international movie festival. Not that I care about those things. To me, a movie is two dollars and a bucket of greasy popcorn whenever I get the free time, which is rarely. But hey, I like movies as much as the next person. Movie stars, on the other hand… Well, when you do what I do for a living, you find out most rich people aren't very nice. Movie stars included. When someone has something of extreme value to protect, like a reputation or a career, they'll do almost anything. Movie stars are like anyone else, except they usually have a lot more to protect.

Anyway, here I am in beautiful Cannes on the eve of the international film festival, and in case I sound like the former soldier I am, I'll admit it's impressive. I can see why so many want to be part of this make-believe world, to sunbathe on those pristine white beaches or stroll down the sidewalk, carrying monogrammed luxury bags. Or be photographed making their way to the seaside parking lot, bristling with yachts.

It's seductive.

That's the problem with wealth: It seduces you into thinking you deserve more than you should have. Fortunately, I've never had much to be seduced by.

As I exit the taxicab and pay the fare in francs, I feel the heat instantly. Only late May and the heat here is never as bad as the humid mid-July swamp-fume of New York City, but it's still intense for this time of year: very dry, like a desert wind that's gotten lazy and decided to take a long nap over the city.

My double-breasted gabardine suit starts itching me even as I turn to the Carlton Hotel. My employer, Lambert Securities, is one of the world's largest insurance firms and insisted I dress the part for this case. Which means they had an expensive suit readied for me before I left London, though it feels as if it's doubled in weight. Usually, I'd have ignored the getup. I'm not here to impress but to do a job that no one else can. But it's a film festival, and the jeweler involved is a very important client— possibly the firm's most important, who just got ripped off for millions of dollars in one-of-a-kind jewels.

Not my crowd. If I can even say my job has a crowd. But, really, not my crowd at all. And the porter in his martinet uniform at the hotel door regards me as if he knows it.

I take a moment to admire the hotel's curvaceous façade and domed turrets. I heard the turrets were designed by an infatuated architect seeking to immortalize the unforgettable endowments of a courtesan named la Belle Otero. Who would have thought? A hotel for the rich and famous, with tits for domes. Only in France.

Inside the lobby, which is cool and glowing with rococo gilding and too much marble, I ask for the hotel manager in my lousy French at the reception desk. I learned the language as well as I needed to do what I did after the war, but the reception staff regards me with the same dubious expression as the doorman. I must look and sound exactly like what I am: a jetlagged American in a new suit, who thinks his French is better than it is.

I flash my license in my wallet. That always catches their attention. The reception guy points me toward a door at the far end of the lobby. As I stride toward it, I swipe my ridiculous new fedora from my head and rake my fingers through my sweat-dampened mop of hair. I should have gotten a decent haircut and shave, along with the suit.

Before I reach the door, a prim man in what looks like a turn-of-the-century morning coat intercepts me. He has the erect posture and slick-backed pate of a long-term bureaucrat—I know the type. And that's what he is, except his bureaucracy is the oversight of this overpriced hotel as he wastes no time in informing me.

"I am Alain Saucey, managing director of the Carlton. Monsieur Curtis, I presume?" He clips out his speech in flawless and slightly accusatory English as if he's aware of my deficiency in the native tongue.

"At your service." I almost smile, only it isn't a smiling occasion. "Lambert Securities sent me."

"I am aware. I called their office in London as soon as the mishap occurred."

Mishap. Now, there's a term I haven't heard before to describe what's happened. Guess the words *heist* or *robbery* don't go over well in sunny Cannes.

"Can you tell me about the…mishap?" I say while he blocks the door behind him.

"I believe those directly involved are best equipped to deliver that information, M. Curtis. I wasn't present. I was attending to our other guests. As you surely must be aware, the festival opens tonight, and we're fully booked. It's very unfortunate, but our guests cannot be unduly disturbed." He pauses. Like most bureaucrats, he's very conscious of his self-importance. "It happened in the back room we reserved for Thorne & Company's exclusive use. Naturally, we're endeavoring to contain the situation to the best of our abilities."

"Right," I say. He keeps looking at me as if he expects me to whip out a notepad and record his declarations for posterity. Containing the situation translates to: I want you to be advised that the Carlton will admit no responsibility. I also have no doubt the hotel's lawyers are busy drafting a ten-page statement to extricate the establishment from any legal culpability. Mishaps like these can be very costly, and the hotel is basically a movie star, too. It has a reputation to protect.

Saucey steps aside to unlock the door, revealing a corridor. "I will escort you. Unless you require my presence, I cannot stay, however. You must understand we're already receiving inquiries from the press." He grimaces. "The vulgarity of today's world."

Word must travel fast here. The mishap is not yet five hours cold, and the vultures are already circling. Which won't make my job any easier.

"The local gendarmes," he goes on as he leads me down the corridor, "are currently questioning members of my staff. As I understand, those directly involved have already given their statements, and word has been dispatched to Paris. They're sending an investigative team, but given the festival, lodgings are, of course, at a premium."

"Is that so?" I say.

This just keeps getting better. An uncooperative hotel manager, already under advice from lawyers to say as little as permissible. Reporters about to swarm the scene. Local police questioning the staff, and the crime bureau in Paris on alert, readying its descent. In less than twenty-four hours, this place will be a circus. "Well, I don't need you present right now," I tell him as he pauses at another door. "But don't wander too far, okay? I may have questions for you later."

He gives me a glance that indicates that my questions, while unwelcome, will be endured if required, and then he opens the door.

The room is small, without windows. I notice that at once. There's this door and another at the other end. "Where does that other door go?" I ask Saucey.

"Into the service area of the hotel," he replies.

"Is that how…?"

He nods, tight-lipped.

I turn to the two people slumped on chairs by an empty table. A man and a woman, both looking queasy. The man holds an icepack to his face, but when he looks up at my approach, he lets out a gasp of recognition. "Curtis?"

It takes a moment before I place him. "Darcy? What the hell…?"

"I could say the same." He rises unsteadily to his feet, all six foot three of him. I didn't recognize him at first because he's put on at least twenty pounds since I last saw him in '48. He thrusts out his hand. "Of all the joints in France," he quips in a faux-Bogart drawl.

I feel how clammy his palm is. "Quite the coincidence. How'd you end up in this mess?"

John Darcy was one of the operatives on my team after the war. While our unexpected reunion is startling, I'm glad to see him. He was always honest. Reliable. And dedicated. Whenever we got word of a potential target, he didn't let up until we had the monster out of his bolt-hole and in a jail cell. No one will ever give him a medal for it—what we did after the war remains top-secret—but if anyone deserves one, it's Darcy. He took down more of those mass-murdering fascists than anyone else. And if our unit hadn't been shut down, he wouldn't have stopped.

"I need to pay my bills," he says, putting the icepack back to his forehead. "You know how it goes. Thorne & Company pays me well, and ex-grunts aren't exactly rolling in dough." He winces. "Can you believe that sonofabitch hit me with chloroform?"

"Chloroform? Are you sure?"

"Yeah, I'm sure. I could smell it. Still can. Like cotton candy. Bastard."

"Damn," I say.

He chuckles. "My head feels like I got hit by a truck. Better than a bullet, I suppose. But, yeah, damn is right. I didn't see a thing." He eases back down on his chair. "And you?"

"Insurance," I say. He meets my eyes. He gets it. This isn't the time or place for long-winded explanations. Besides, he knows as well as I do that's the least of what I do. Insurance is my cover. My skills go far beyond it. Like his.

I turn my attention to the woman. "I'm from Lambert Securities, Thorne & Company's insurance firm. Do you speak any English, Miss…?"

She nods. "Sylvia Morton. I'm Miss Thorne's personal assistant."

"Did you see the culprit, Miss Morton?"

"Yes. He—he came in after Mr. Darcy delivered the cases. We were waiting for—"

"Our boss," Darcy cuts in. He swallows. "Ania Thorne. She's the only one with the codes."

"Codes?" I understand what he means, but I want to hear it from him.

"Yeah. You know. Numeric codes. Each case has one. Unique, no two alike. She always unlocks the cases herself. But before she got here, he hit me with the chloroform."

"And then?" I return my gaze to the woman, who casts a worried look at John. It's obvious to me they're involved somehow and trying to hide it. The boss's personal assistant and the security detail making nookie… Not what you'd call professional behavior.

"He just walked in." Her voice is barely a whisper. "He had a gun. He pointed me into that corner and took the cases."

"Six minutes," Darcy says. "The bastard did it in six goddamn minutes!"

"Did he say anything?" I ask her.

She shakes her head.

"What was he wearing?"

"All black. A mask. Like…like a ski mask. Gloves."

"What kind of gloves?"

She hesitates. "Normal? They were black, too. I'm sorry, it happened so fast…"

Normal. Black. Not what I'm hoping to hear. One of the Leopard's signature stunts is flaunting leopard-print gloves during his heists; it's how he earned his moniker and captured public attention. But it's been six years since his last job in London, and that went very wrong. He's kept a low profile since, but only because he made his first mistake. To me, this new heist bears his trademarks: Fast. Efficient. Executed to perfection. All witnesses left alive.

Except for the gloves. That's a shift. After the blunder in London, did he lose some of his bravura if none of his nerve?

"It was him, wasn't it?" says Darcy, breaking into my thoughts. Gotta hand it to him. He was never slow on the uptake. "The Leopard?"

Sylvia Morton lets out a little moan of dismay.

"I don't know yet," I say. "How much did he take?"

"Everything." She passes a trembling hand over her face. "All of it. Every jewel we brought for the festival. I don't have the list here."

"Why not?"

"He took it. It was by one of the cases."

"But not the codes." I glance at Darcy again. Chloroform is nasty; it can kill in the right dose. And he's a big guy. Yet the thief knew exactly how much to use to knock him out. If it's the Leopard, he's playing by the rules this time. No unexpected blunders.

Darcy coughs. "God, I feel like crap. No, not the codes. I told you, only Miss Thorne has them. By the time she got here, it was over. She alerted the hotel."

"No one has reported finding the cases yet," I say, recalling the report Lambert compiled for me. "He vanished. How does one man, dressed all in black, walk out of a fully booked hotel at seven-fifteen in the morning with seven locked cases of jewels?"

Darcy shrugs his meaty shoulders. "Beats me. I mean, I never even heard him come up behind me, Jerome. I swear it. And you know damn well that's not normal for me."

"No," I say. "It's not." Darcy might be a tank, but even in his less muscular days on our team, he had the stealth of a cat. I can still remember how we stalked one of the Dachau butchers, alerted that he was trying to cross the border into Poland. Darcy crept up to that bombed-out basement in total silence. Before the butcher could yank out his pistol, Darcy was on top of him, pounding his Nazi mug into the dirt.

"Is this the usual procedure?" I ask. "Bring the cases into a strange room and wait for Miss Thorne to open them? Why not do it in her suite, where it's safer?"

Darcy gives me a baffled look as if the thought never occurred to him. I'm disappointed. Though it's not his call, is it? In my years doing this work, I've seen all sorts of inexplicable behavior from the very people who should know better. It's only reinforced my belief that the rich rely too much on their privilege and not enough on common sense. Like the war. Jews with money thought it would all blow over if they waited long enough, until it became clear it wouldn't. Only then did they try to get out. It's how it goes. The rich always think they have all the time in the world. Until they don't.

"We always open a temporary shop in the hotel," Sylvia says. "To exhibit the jewels during the festival. This is the room we chose, but we had to inspect the pieces first."

"Why?"

"Mr. Curtis, those jewels are the finest Thorne & Company has to offer, many of them brand-new designs. Some of them had been designated for celebrities to wear at the opening gala, so Miss Thorne had appointments scheduled all afternoon. Designations can change at a moment's notice. A celebrity sees the jewels we chose for her and decides she doesn't like them. Ania—Miss Thorne—prefers to not open the cases in her suite because…"

"Because?"

Sylvia hesitates. I can see it's not because she wants to keep the information from me but that she's afraid for her job—as she should be, given the circumstances.

"Miss Morton. Nothing you tell me will go past the necessary parties. Lambert insured those pieces for a considerable sum, so I need to know as much as possible."

She sighs. "Actresses can be so competitive."

"As in, they might demand to see everything you brought and want to wear another actress's selection?"

"Yes. By inspecting the pieces here, no one else sees them but us. Miss Thorne can make any changes before we take each selection to her suite for her appointments."

"Leaving only Darcy here to guard the other pieces?"

"The cases are always relocked," retorts Darcy. "I have a gun." He thrusts open his jacket to reveal the holstered weapon. "Look here. If you're suggesting—"

I hold up my hand. "Simmer down, John. I'm not suggesting anything. It's just unusual. A lot of very expensive loot to leave with just one man, capable as he is."

"Yeah, well, this isn't a usual event, is it? It's a movie festival with Elizabeth goddamn Taylor and Sophia Loren. Those dames aren't about to be outdone by each other's tiaras."

Sylvia shoots him a look. "John, please." She gives me a cautious smile. "It is unusual, I'll admit. But Miss Thorne specifically instructed it be done this way. She had the hotel's full assurance this room would be safe. Darcy was stationed outside the door you came through at all times. We were to use the other door and take the service lift to her suite. No one ever imagined with the festival about to open, and the hotel staff about…" Her voice drifts off as she realizes what she's just admitted.

"In my experience," I tell her, "not imagining the worst is how the worst happens." I don't add that it should be Darcy's experience, too. He was with me after the war. He saw the worst with his own eyes and how thousands of people let it happen because they never imagined it could.

Darcy makes an exasperated sound. He knows he screwed up. As Thorne's security detail, he should have raised the objection, even if he risked his well-paying job. But I also know how tough it was for all of us when the military disbanded our team without explanation, though we later found out our government had made an agreement with the Allies to not dispatch American agents on their own to hunt down war criminals. A mistake. Many of those we could have brought to justice went underground to escape during the chaos, while the Allies hammered out their treaties and divvied up the goods. More of those thugs would have ended up in Nuremberg if we'd been allowed to do our job. Instead, we were transferred to other sections or discharged to seek employment elsewhere, forewarned never to reveal our former occupation. We lost touch with each other. On purpose. We distanced ourselves from what we'd seen and done, even if none of us ever forgot it.

Some things you just couldn't forget.

As I consider all of this, Darcy says, "Still the same old Lieutenant Curtis."

"Excuse me?" I stare at him.

He chuckles. "Now, who needs to simmer down? I meant you're recording all of this in that machine of yours you call a brain. Not a single written note."

"Notes can be misplaced," I reply. "And you should get that meat-head of yours checked out by a doctor. You look awful."

He grimaces.

I say to Sylvia, "I'll need to speak with Miss Thorne. Where can I find her?"

"In her suite." Sylvia stands, nervously straightening her pencil skirt. A pretty woman. Wholesome as an English rose. Darcy always did have an eye for the ladies. "She's very busy, I'm afraid. The theft…she has to explain it to our clients."

"All those competitive actresses," I clarify, and as she nods, the queasy look returns to her face. I add, "I have to do something first. John,"—I glance at him before I move to the door—"see a doctor. I mean it."

"Yes, lieutenant," he growls sarcastically.

In the corridor, I take a moment to calm myself. Then I march toward the lobby and, what do you know? M. Alain Saucey pops up out of nowhere, just as I thought he would.

"*Oui?*" he barks, without any inflection to mar his may-I-help-you, sir? tone.

"The cases." I don't temper my tone of voice now.

He's a cool customer; I'll give him that. He doesn't even look surprised. "Cases?"

I take a step closer to him. "The jewelry cases." I let a moment of silence pass as he meets my stare and gets the message that I'm not going to take any crap from him. When he doesn't say anything, I do. "I don't know about France, but in Great Britain and the United States, withholding information from an insurance investigator is a prosecutable offense."

He moves backward, reasserting the distance between us in more ways than one. "I was specifically instructed by the police—"

"I don't care. Lambert Securities is facing an insurance claim in the high millions because of this hotel's negligence."

"Negligence!" Now, I get the reaction I want. "How dare you—?"

"Where are the hotel security guards? Do you even have any? I won't ask about undercover because I already know the answer. But a visible guard or two? With all these famous guests who mustn't be disturbed?"

He turns stiff as a flagpole. "The Carlton is one of the most respected establishments in Cannes. Our guests come here because they value their privacy and our discretion."

"Right. It would be vulgar for your discreet establishment to hire security guards during an international film festival, so your valued guests don't get robbed at gunpoint, is that it?" When I see the pallor creep across his already colorless face, I go on. "Miss Thorne is one of those valued guests, isn't she?"

He glares at me. I welcome it. I want to get his reptile blood up.

"The cases," I repeat.

His mouth tightens. Just as I think I might have to show him my holstered weapon under my jacket, he says through clenched teeth, "They were located in a laundry basket by a service exit. Empty."

"All seven?"

"Yes."

"Show me this service exit."

The exit opens onto an alleyway lined with waste bins. The laundry basket was left inside by the door, heaped with sheets, towels, and tablecloths to be laundered. He buried the cases under the soiled fabric and went through the alleyway—which I ascertain gives way to a decorative wrought-iron gate that a six-year-old child could clamber over—and onto the promenade girdling the private beach maintained by the hotel for its guests.

Smoking a much-needed cigarette as I walk from the exit through the alleyway to the fence, I check my wristwatch. It took him less than five minutes. He stashed the jewels in another container, a valise perhaps, like a notary or solicitor, and disappeared on the promenade, crowded with beachgoers and early morning shoppers. He might have changed his clothes to blend in. Or maybe not. The promenade ends at that impressive yacht parking lot, but he probably had a car parked nearby. No need to walk any farther than necessary.

In a mere eleven minutes, he robbed one of the world's most renowned jewelers and made off with enough loot to bankrupt the company. And no one but Sylvia Morton caught a glimpse of him. I could canvas every person who was on the promenade at around that time, and I bet no one would recollect seeing anything unusual.

Because that's how he does it. How he's always done it. The trick, as it were, is not to be hasty. To not stand out at all. A man carrying a valise, going somewhere in the morning on the eve of a film festival; he could be anyone.

Except I know better. The Leopard did this. No one else could have done it.

And he somehow obtained the codes to unlock the cases before leaving the hotel. How, if only the company director knew the codes? I have to consider the possibility of an inside job. Someone on Thorne & Company's payroll, who was bribed or threatened. I can't imagine Darcy falling prey to blackmail or financial temptation, but as he said, grunts aren't rolling in dough, so anything is possible. And the lovely Miss Morton looked very upset, of course, but…she might have looked that way for another reason.

One thing is certain: Someone close to Miss Thorne likely gave the Leopard those codes. Unless she was careless, which I doubt. I've read her dossier, provided by the insurance firm. She's not the type to be careless.

Ania Thorne is twenty-eight years old, nine years younger than me, and she's been designing the Thorne & Company collections since she was nineteen. Very well-educated and fluent in several languages, she apprenticed under Cartier before joining her father's company as lead designer. Virgil Thorne, known as *Jeweler to the Stars*, was becoming infamous for his tirades against his clients for failing to pay their bills, as the rich tend to do, costing his company millions in lawsuits. Ania turned all of it around—no mean feat. After his board ousted him, Virgil's daughter surged to the forefront as the company's new director. She mended long-standing rifts with clients, introduced modern eccentricities like belted saffron diamonds and serpentine ruby clasps; insectoid topazes with emerald-tipped antennae; and other rarities that proved extremely profitable. From well-heeled socialites on Fifth Avenue to the garish wives of studio heads in Beverly Hills, no woman's wardrobe is deemed complete without a Thorne & Company piece. Preferably several if you could afford it—which few can.

No, she doesn't strike me as the careless type. But I'll soon find out.

I brace myself for the ensuing drama as I step off the elevator into a beige-upholstered hallway leading to embossed double doors. A very distraught jeweler awaits me inside that suite, probably in no mood for questions—which Miss Morton seems to confirm when she asks me to wait outside while she knocks quietly on the doors, then slips past them at an unheard cue.

After several minutes of waiting, I detect the surge of raised voices and decide to ignore the formalities. Going through the doors into a sun-flooded suite larger than my London flat, all done up in blue and gold, I see two women by a marble fireplace—that's right, they apparently have fireplaces in five-star hotel suites—and feel Miss Morton's urgent clasp of my elbow, hear her whisper at my ear. "Please, allow her a moment. She's with a very important client."

I pause by the entry to the living area. One of the women is petite, her short dark hair in waves, her voluptuous figure encased in a pleated white dress. She's also very angry. I can hear her. Not much, but enough. She has a piercing voice as she flings up her arms in a gesture of disgust. To my eyes, it looks practiced, almost staged.

The other woman is taller by nearly a head. Her back is to me as she faces the enraged one, but wow…there's a sight I don't see every day. Very slim in a tailored grey skirt and fitted jacket with a flare at the hips, ash-blond hair drawn into a knot at her nape, shapely legs with defined calves sheathed in translucent hose and grey satin pumps. She must be the client, patiently enduring the injured jeweler's incredulous tirade, at a loss to explain how Madame Movie Star's designated tiara, necklace, and bracelet won't be available for tonight's gala.

Then, as Miss Morton draws me farther aside, the woman in the white dress whirls toward us, declaring hotly, "Next time, I'll just bring *my own* jewels!"

I freeze. The woman's flashing violet-blue eyes rake over me as she storms past, flinging open the cream-colored double doors to depart in a tempest of perfume and hauteur. I recognize her famous face, despite its fury.

Elizabeth goddamned Taylor.

The blonde raises a hand. Miss Morton immediately slips off into the hallway, where I hear her low-voiced attempt to reassure the enraged Miss Taylor.

I move into the living area. The woman turns to me from the fireplace.

Now, let me be clear. I see a lot of beautiful things in my job. The jewels, certainly. Even if I'm no connoisseur, they are always exquisite: the way their colors capture the light in multi-faceted depths, the allure they exude from their elaborate settings as if they're not lifeless stones but the eyes of a supreme goddess. I've heard jewelers' laments as they mourn the theft of their creations as if they've lost a child. I've seen the sensitive fingertips that coaxed the reluctant gems from their unpolished prison, the keen hands that sheared and shaped the deity into an adornment fit for queens.

But I never let myself get drawn in. I can't. When the goddess vanishes, and I know the chances of recovering her are slim to none, I can't be personally involved. My job is to investigate how she was taken and determine who coveted her. My job is to sort through the events leading up to her disappearance, all the conflicting facts, and, in time, if I'm lucky—and I'm usually not—hunt her down, just as I once hunted Nazis in post-war wreckage. My job is to find her and return her—if I can—so she can be sold to her paying master. Beauty has no part in it, and the jewel doesn't care. Like every goddess, it only requires worship. Queen or thief, it makes no difference. That's her seduction and her deceit. As long as she receives her due homage, she'll shine for anyone who possesses her.

Yet I now feel almost paralyzed as the flesh-and-blood goddess before me regards me with icy skepticism. Yes, she could definitely be a movie star. She has that magnetic air, the aura of a life lived high above the rest of us. Though as I meet her cool, grey-blue eyes, almost jewel-like themselves in the angular face with its high cheekbones and flawless skin, her attitude does not invite movie star flattery. I see no sign of distraught victim here. Of course, she's the head of a world-famous company. She's had to perfect her public façade. But my God…the woman makes it hard to breathe.

Get it together, Curtis.

As she extends her tapered hand with its blunt nails—the appendage of a practicing jeweler—I see the years of struggle to reach where she is. The ambition and self-control she's had to harness to overcome the inevitable scheming behind her back, the callous remarks that no woman can succeed in this business, much less follow in Virgil Thorne's footsteps, and her determination to prove them wrong. She may not have known a moment's deprivation in her life, but that doesn't mean it's been easy.

And now, all of it lost in less than eleven minutes of overconfidence in a hotel, lacking adequate security. All of it searing in her crystal-cool voice as she says, "I understand you're the investigator. So, tell me, Mr. Curtis. How does someone dare steal from *me?*"

Chapter Two

Ania

My father's voice is in my head as I extend my hand to the man in front of me.

Show no emotion, Ania.

Being in charge, retaining your power in any given situation requires that your opponent never know what affects you. What thrills or scares you, what you despise or desire, is all private information people can use against you. At one time, I thought my father paranoid for instilling these lessons in me.

Now, I know he was being prudent.

There's an ugly underside to my world. Under the flowerbed rich with roses and irises, the earth seethes with snakes. My father taught me more than how to appreciate jewels, more than how to design an irresistible piece, how to select the perfect gemstone and evaluate what precious metal works best for it. He also taught me the value of recognizing duplicity. Of always being suspicious. Of knowing that taking care of business is looking out for myself and the company before anything else.

I've also learned that nothing gives a client the idea they can take advantage of you faster than seeing your blood pulse in your neck or the sheen of anxiety on your forehead. So, I extend my hand to this stranger and hold back from blurting out how afraid I am, how worried about the repercussions of this disaster to both me and Thorne & Company.

As he shakes my hand, I find myself oddly aware of how much larger his palm is than mine. How warm against the coolness of my fingers. Even when everyone else finds the weather too hot, I'm never uncomfortable. Friends joke that my body temperature must be several degrees colder than a person's ought to be.

It's the ice, my father once told me. We have diamond dust in our blood, and it keeps us cold.

I control my breathing, clear my head, and look the man in the eyes as I try to block out the echo of Elizabeth Taylor's screeching as it fades from the outside hallway.

"I understand you're the insurance company investigator. So, tell me, Mr. Curtis, how does someone dare steal from *me*?"

"A question I hope to answer, Miss Thorne." His voice is calm, a bit hoarse. As if he's tired or smokes too much. But it reassures me. At least on first impression, he doesn't appear someone prone to hasty conclusions or panic.

"I hope for exactly the same thing," I reply. "I'm pleased to hear we're in agreement."

The man's deep-set, hazel eyes are somber as he meets my gaze. "I assumed you'd want a speedy solution. Or we wouldn't be in agreement."

Clouds shift over the sun outside, casting us in shadow for a moment so I can no longer see his expression.

"I am sorry, however, to be meeting under these circumstances," he adds.

"To say the least. Now, please have a seat. Tell me what progress you've made." I indicate the space opposite me at the table by the window. The inspector folds his lanky frame into the chair in a fluid motion. I expected less gracefulness from such a tall man, though he's also quite thin for his height, his suit hanging on him like an afterthought.

"How soon before I can expect to have my jewels back?" I ask, slightly impatient as he takes his time.

One of his thick eyebrows arches. "I don't have any leads yet, Miss Thorne. I only arrived an hour ago. I know you're under constraints. So am I. The more you can answer for me, the better chance I have of finding the perpetrator and your jewels."

He's not saying what I want to hear. I sneak a furtive glance at my watch.

"Miss Morton told me you don't have much time for this interview," he says.

He's observant. Good. Exactly what one should want in an investigator, I imagine. I've never had to deal with one before. We've never been robbed. We've been very fortunate in that regard. So many other jewelers have suffered serious losses over the years. But it seems our luck has run out.

"As I told your assistant," Mr. Curtis goes on, "I can't complete the investigation in a limited amount of time. Hopefully, you'll allow me as long as it takes to gather the necessary facts. After all, these are millions of dollars we're talking about, right?"

I look over at Sylvia. "Who is my next appointment with?"

"Miss Hepburn at one-thirty," she says.

While the star is known for her gentility, she's still a celebrity, a valued client, and must be treated as such. "Can you please call her and explain? Tell her what I tried to tell Miss Taylor: that I contacted our store in New York as soon as I discovered what happened, and they're sending over replacements. They will be here by the time the festival opens. Not for tonight's gala, unfortunately. But as soon as the jewelry arrives, we'll arrange to bring pieces to her—"

"Replacements?" interjects Mr. Curtis.

"Yes." I return my gaze to him. "I've had to request pieces from our New York vault. Not the same, of course. Everything I brought here was original, created especially for this event. But our company has a history, so I requested some of our iconic past pieces. I'll spin a new theme around them—maybe a focus on classics…" I realize I'm brainstorming with the insurance investigator, which is inappropriate. What made me think he'd be interested in my solution? I stop explaining to return to the information he actually needs. "I'm free until the replacements arrive. Which, as I said, should be in…"

I glance at my watch again. It is the only piece of jewelry I wear, an oddity that endless newspaper columns have remarked on. How can a woman who spends her life creating fantastic jewelry wear none? It's not for lack of interest. I'm in awe of the stones. I bow to them. Respect them. Adore them. I fall in love with every stone I work with. I become emotionally involved with every piece. But my creation is meant for someone else to fall in love with. I do have some of the pieces my father made for my mother. I sometimes put them on in private, remembering how I watched her get dressed to go out for the evening. I'd perch on her plush bed while she sat at her dressing table, touching perfume to her wrists. Patting her face with powder. Highlighting her lashes with mascara. And then looking through her jewelry case to pick out what she planned to wear that night. She always called me over.

"Come, Ania. What do you think goes best with this dress?"

Since I refuse to play favorites with my pieces, I wear none. Just the watch my mother owned before she met my father. A Cartier tank, circa 1910. Inscribed on the back are her initials and the date of her college graduation. I close my eyes for a moment, abruptly overwhelmed by the grief of missing her, even after so many years.

Sylvia returns from making the call I requested. "Miss Hepburn's assistant says she understands and will wait. Is there anything else I can do?"

"Thank goodness. Yes, please talk to Miss Taylor's people. She didn't stay here long enough for me to let her know we'll have more pieces by tomorrow. Offer her one of them as our gift to make up for the inconvenience. That should satisfy her."

I wince inwardly as I say this. We can't afford to give away jewelry worth tens of thousands of dollars. But neither can we afford this setback. Headlines about the largest jewel heist Cannes has ever seen are hardly the press I'd hoped for when I set out on this trip. I'd anticipated glowing articles with a dateline from film festival beside photos of our creations, worn by the most luminous women in Hollywood.

"Ania, is there anything you need before I go to Miss Taylor's suite?" Sylvia asks.

I could use some coffee. I've been operating on fumes. No rest. No food. No good news. I need a jolt of caffeine.

"Would you like some coffee, Mr. Curtis?" I say.

He gives an eager nod. "Sure. I've been traveling all day. No breakfast. Once the call came in, there was no time to waste."

I surmised as much from his rumpled suit, the ragged look of someone who's been cramped in an airplane for hours—living in the clouds as I call it. Some people find it terrifying. For others, it's but a necessary evil. I love it. I've taken lessons and can fly my own plane. Between our two offices in Beverly Hills and New York City, it's convenient for me to take myself, though the company board insists on a pilot. They deem my penchant for flying unattended an unnecessary risk.

"Then perhaps you'd like more than coffee? The Carlton is famous for their club sandwiches. May I tempt you?"

I see him hesitate.

"Is eating on the job not allowed? Please, don't worry about breaking a few rules if we can do all of this in less time. I won't report you to your boss."

A smile inches across his mouth. To my surprise, he has an unexpectedly warm smile, like his hands. It changes his face, which is weathered and has a dark five o'clock shadow; the visage of a man who, despite the obviously new—if wrinkled—suit, has no vanity.

"All right. Sure," he says. "If you'll join me."

"That's a good idea, Ania," Sylvia adds. She knows I haven't eaten since last night.

"A salad for me, please." I turn back to him. "Now, how long do you expect the investigation to take?" I ask, as Sylvia places the order with room service and proceeds to Miss Taylor's suite.

"That's an impossible question to answer right now." He actually chuckles.

"Mr. Curtis, my company's reputation is at stake. A reputation I've devoted the last five years of my life to restoring."

I'm immediately annoyed at myself. I've just admitted that my company had a serious problem in the past. Which means I've obviously not yet taken in what happened this morning. I need to be careful. But I'm facing a terrible situation, so I'm not even sure what I should be more upset about. That people in my employ could have been seriously injured or killed, or that pieces I spent months perfecting—with each client in mind—for our first return to Cannes since the board forced out my father are gone? *Oh, stop fooling yourself.* I know what upsets me the most. My lost jewelry. My one-of-a-kind pieces. I agonized over their designs. Every creation took hundreds of hours. First, as I designed it on paper. Then as I sourced each stone. I chose the pearls, the diamonds, tourmalines, rubies, emeralds, sapphires, opals, and peridots. Every gem contains a bit of magic. My father first taught me that when I was a girl, when my dolls had real pearl necklaces made up in the Thorne workroom and miniature couture outfits created by Dior as a favor to Papa. My marbles were gem-quality onyx, quartz, and amethyst. My bedroom had Impressionist artwork on the walls. Everything in my life prepared me to be who I am: my father's heir. He wanted a son. He still jokes about it sometimes, though now he says he can't imagine that any man would have stepped into his shoes better than I did. Laughing and looking down at my high-heel-clad feet, telling me no son would have the audacity to wear nothing but Roger Vivier exclusively, either.

If he harbors any lingering disappointment, he hides it well.

You're your father's daughter was the refrain in our house. My mother would shake her head in chagrin to find me holed up in my father's library at six years old, seated at his desk, sketching. Not blue skies, green grass, and stick-figure families, but pieces of jewelry I conjured out of my imagination.

Mr. Curtis says, "I want to go over everything that happened from the time you arrived in Cannes with the pieces to the events of this morning, Miss Thorne."

"Certainly."

"First, a few facts. Other than Darcy and Miss Morton, who else knew where the jewelry cases were stored?"

"I did. And I assume whoever is in charge of hotel security."

"And on your end?"

"No one else but us."

He takes a moment as if mulling this over. Then he says, "I'm aware you're in a very competitive business. Are any of your competitors more ruthless than others? Anyone you've had questionable dealings with? In other words, any enemies, Miss Thorne?"

I am taken aback. A rarity for me. "Why would you ask that?"

"Because this is a particularly high-profile theft. Not just the jewels themselves but also the opportunity for international press and scandal," he replies dryly.

I don't appreciate his tone. Has he failed to take into account my personal loss in all this? Then I realize I'm losing my self-control. My personal loss is of no concern to him.

"Yes," I say. "Precisely. Dressing stars in our jewelry is one of the most important public-relation efforts we make. To have pictures of Miss Loren, Miss Taylor, Miss Hepburn, and others in the newspapers and magazines, wearing our jewels, is essential to our image and marketing campaigns."

"Who runs those campaigns?"

"I do."

"Not an outside advertising agency?"

"I work with one who buys our media, but I'm responsible for the creative."

"Why is that?"

"To maintain full control over our image. Image is everything in our business."

And the line I created for this season would go farther than any other in reinforcing that image as an innovative, lasting force. An image the board charged me to repair after years of my father's mismanagement.

"As for enemies," I go on, "I'm unaware of anyone in particular who'd do this. But it's the jewelry business. No one likes anyone to do better than them. I'm sure the opportunity for us to dress the stars in our jewels for the festival didn't please our competitors."

Mr. Curtis lets another moment pass. "Tell me about the pieces for the festival."

"Well, the theme was heavenly bodies. The earrings for Miss Taylor were moons in various phases with gems set in platinum. Platinum bangle bracelets for Miss Loren with diamond stars. For Miss Hepburn, I designed a suite of a pearl necklace of moonstone and diamond stars with a matching bracelet. I also designed rings of the zodiac signs to be worn stacked. There were a dozen other special pieces. A ruby brooch and matching earrings suggesting Saturn. A gold and yellow diamond parure featuring the sun..."

My voice fades. The investigator regards me with...not exactly amusement, but a more elusive quality. As if he's seen through me, detected the inadvertent fire in my voice as I describe what I've lost.

"I see. When I met with Mr. Darcy and Miss Morton downstairs, they explained the procedure for opening the cases and showed me where the cases had been brought from the hotel vault." He pauses. "Am I right in assuming the cases were stored in the vault from the hour of your arrival in the hotel until the events of this morning?"

"Of course," I reply, more indignantly than I probably should. I measure my tone. "Is Mr. Darcy feeling better? I am very concerned about his condition."

"Darcy's tough," Mr. Curtis replies. I think he might chuckle again, but he doesn't. "Only he could get right back up after a dose of chloroform. It can be hard to recover from, and he'll have a serious headache, but in the long run, he'll be fine."

"Sylvia said she saw the man. Does that help you?"

"Her description didn't include anything very specific," he says.

I clasp my hands together in my lap. "This is a nightmare," I hear myself say.

"It is. But I must admit, you seem very calm about it."

Is that suspicion in his voice? I'm not sure.

"Mr. Curtis, I'm the victim here."

"I'm just stating it as I see it."

"Yes, well. I'm very good at presenting a stoic exterior, even when I'm not. It's an ability I've had to develop. May we continue?"

He leans forward in his chair, his eyes intent on me. I find it distracting. He has the kind of focus that misses nothing. And I don't like being examined. I get a hint of scent from him—common yet intriguing. A touch of pine. From the dried and mostly extinct pomade on that disheveled mass of dark brown hair? He must have used pomade at some point. Men usually do—even those without vanity, who need a haircut.

"Miss Thorne, I'm not here to make this uncomfortable," he says at length. "But to do my job, I need your full cooperation. Anything that you think of—no matter how small or insignificant it might seem. Often, it's the little things that crack open cases like this."

"How many cases like this have you cracked open, Mr. Curtis?" I ask.

His face shifts, and for a second, I see something disturbing under his stoic façade. A hidden anger. I recognize it. I have it, too.

He doesn't answer me. "Let's go over your movements from yesterday to today."

"Why? Am I now a suspect?" Because he's starting to treat me as if I might be.

"Not that I'm aware of—" he starts to say, but I interrupt him.

"Because if I am, you should ask yourself why I'd want to destroy my own reputation. Do you have any idea how much time and effort I've spent building this company to bring it back? My father founded it. The company is his legacy. His life's work."

"I do. In fact, Lambert Securities provided me with a dossier on both you and your company that it keeps fully up to date. As it does with all of its clients. I assume you must do the same with yours."

"Well, then you hold an advantage over me. I don't have a dossier on you. How do I even know you're the right man for the job?"

"With all due respect, Miss Thorne, I'm the only man for the job."

He sounds very confident. Is it true? I'm tempted to ask what would happen if I telephoned the insurance company and requested background information on him.

"Why is that?" I say instead.

"Because I'm the man Lambert hires for crimes like this. And for the record, I don't work for you. I work for Lambert, your insurance firm. If I can recover these jewels, I'll be saving my employer a payout of millions of dollars in claims on those pieces."

"So, my company and I benefit by default?" I'm not certain why I'm doing this, why I feel this urge to needle him. Only that he's acting as if this is something that goes on every day. As if it's routine to endure and accommodate. And while it perhaps happens often enough in his world, it certainly does *not* in mine.

Once more ignoring my question, he says, "Can you tell me where you were last night?"

I resign myself to reciting my schedule, explaining that I never fraternize with my clients or attend the parties the film festival is well known for.

"I arrived in the late afternoon from Paris on my plane. I was very tired. I don't care about the fêtes. I'm here to work. And that's what I did. After I made sure everything was prepared for today, I ordered a pot of chamomile tea and was in bed by ten o'clock. I had a very busy day ahead of me. You can confirm this with Miss Morton. She was with me from the time we landed in Cannes until I sent her to her room for the night. She returned here early this morning to consult with me before heading downstairs to oversee the removal of the cases from the vault with Mr. Darcy."

And that's when it hits me. For the first time. All of my beautiful pieces are missing. Gone. Maybe lost forever. All those long months of painstaking work, of pouring my heart into them. I know from the moment I sit down at my drawing board that my jewels don't belong to me. I am their muse, their creator, but they belong to someone else. Another woman will put them on her skin to be admired and revered. Their fate is hers, not mine. Yet despite this, I also know that you can't remove the creator from her creations. The time spent lost in wonder, unaware of hunger or thirst. The white-hot frenzy that's nothing like anything else I've experienced. That's how I expect sex to be, yet it never is. When I design, I'm in a world apart. And once the gems have been sourced, the molds prepared, and the piece created, once I hold it in my hands, I know that it belongs to me in a way that selling it can never break. But to have it stolen from me? It feels like a violation of my very soul.

Mr. Curtis is asking me something.

"I'm sorry, what did you say?"

"I said, are you all right, Miss Thorne?"

What emotion have I inadvertently shown him?

"Yes, of course. I'm fine."

"I was asking if you have any pictures of the pieces."

I nod. "We always photograph them alone and in combination with each other, so I can suggest to each client various ways to wear them."

"Could you show me these photographs?"

Is it my imagination, or do I now hear something provocative in his voice? Another subtle intimation that while I may not be a suspect, I've somehow been lax, done or not done something that allowed the theft to happen? I'm starting to resent Mr. Curtis and his x-ray eyes, rumpled suit, and cheap pine pomade.

I walk to the desk to retrieve my portfolio. For a moment, I glance out the window. My tenth-floor suite overlooks the bay. The sun sparkling on the azure waters turns it into a velvet wrap studded in diamonds and sapphires. The view makes me want to cry. I had such high hopes for this trip, such anticipation, imagining my new designs on the stars I've courted and convinced to give me the chance to make them shine.

No. No. No. I suck in a breath. I can't show more emotion than I already have. Can't reveal how distraught I am. How anxious and worried. How…vulnerable.

But Mr. Curtis senses it. "Miss Thorne, would you like me to get you a glass of water?"

I set the portfolio before him. "Please. Go on with your…questions."

A knock sounds on the door. Sylvia hasn't returned from Miss Taylor's suite, so I answer it. One of the hotel's waitstaff is in the hallway with a wheeled, linen-draped tray. On it is a large silver carafe of coffee and domed silver dishes—service for two.

The waiter asks if I'd like him to serve. I decline. Time is ticking. If I do it, it will take only a moment. The waiter would likely make a grand show of it.

The gentleman lets himself out. By the time I hear the door click shut, I have the coffee poured. Then I lift the dome of Mr. Curtis's sandwich. The warm smell of bacon wafts up.

I attend to my plate. When I lift the silver dome and look down, I find an envelope. Opening it, a diamond and moonstone necklace tumbles onto my salad.

"Oh, God." I reel backwards with a gasp. As sudden faintness overcomes me, I fight it down. For the first time since the theft, I've finally lost the last shreds of my composure, but I refuse to drop in a swoon at Mr. Curtis's scuffed feet.

He bolts up and out of his chair with a burst of speed that belies his former languid movements. All of a sudden, he's tense, coiled like a wire about to spring. He leans to my plate. Goes still. "Is this one of the…?" he says in a very low voice.

"Yes," I whisper.

"There's a note." After a seemingly interminable moment, he extricates it from under the lettuce and hands it to me without reading it.

I force my eyes to focus on the handwritten message. I read it aloud:

It's one thing for Liz and Sophia to find other adornments, but it would be a crime if Audrey wore anything but a Thorne on her neck.

Chapter Three

Jerome

She looks as if she might faint. She doesn't have much in the way of color to start with, way too pale except for her temperamental eyes, but now she appears ashen. I want to hold out my hand, as much to steady her as to examine the note she's just read before I race out the door to question the waiter who delivered the room service.

Then she lifts her face to me, and I see she's not going to faint at all.

She's ashen, yes. With rage. She may have developed a stoic exterior for the sake of business, but I've deduced how personal business is to her. She spoke of her jewels as if they were loved ones. I've heard similar sentiments in the past after the shock of a theft, but I still found myself moved by how she described what are, in the end, objects meant to be sold and profited by. Objects worth more than most working-class people earn in a lifetime and often valued over human lives. Objects that, for all their outward beauty, can cause untold misery, too. Misery she's just experienced firsthand. I've heard similar sentiments, but none as heartfelt as hers. Ania Thorne loves her work far more than she probably should.

"What on earth…?" She thrusts the note at me as if it scalded her.

I look it over. "Do you recognize the handwriting?"

"No." Her voice sounds as if she has a pebble lodged in her throat.

"But the necklace is one of yours, stolen this morning?"

"Yes. One of the pieces I designed for Miss Hepburn." She strides suddenly to the picture window overlooking the movie set bay. I see her short-nailed hand press to the immaculate glass. "This must be a very sick joke of some kind."

"I'll say." I realize in that moment that we both touched the note. Bad move. It should be dusted for fingerprints. I flip open her portfolio, rip out a plastic-covered sheet with a photograph of a tiara or something equally ornate, remove the photo, and tuck in the note.

"Do you mind? Those photographs are my personal property."

I look up to find her staring at me. Oh, yeah. She has a temper under that frosty exterior. "Fingerprints," I explain. "I have to be sure, though I doubt it. Not his style."

None of this is his style, actually, but as I realize I've just made another bad move—*what* is it about her? She's making it very tough for me to do my job—she says coldly, "Not his style? I thought you had no leads, Mr. Curtis."

The silence between us turns heavy. Then, as I reach into my pocket for my cigarettes and lighter, she moves toward me. "What aren't you telling me?" Her eyes drop to the cigarette package in my hand. "Go ahead."

I belatedly offer my crumpled pack of Chesterfields.

"No, thank you. I don't smoke." She returns to her seat, regarding my untouched sandwich and the cups of coffee in disgust. Then she sets the dome back on her plate with the necklace still on the salad and pushes it aside.

"If you're hungry, eat mine," I offer.

"I've lost my appetite." She leans back a little on her chair, crossing those stunning legs. "You were saying? Or *not* saying, as the case may be? About *his* style?"

I blow out smoke. *Well, Jerome, fine sling you've just put your ass in.* I never inform my clients, or Lambert's to be more precise, of the details of my investigation, especially this early in the process. Not only because I need time to gather all the relevant facts, as I assured her earlier, but because it's cruel to dangle hope when, in reality, there's rarely anything to hope for. She aimed her question about how many cases I've cracked open right at my gut. Because the answer is none, at least not where the Leopard is concerned. I've never recovered anything he's taken. Not one item. I know nothing about him either, except how he operates.

But there's no avoiding it now. There's the note and returned necklace: a taunt if ever I've seen one. None of it is his style, but I can't evade the facts staring me in the face like she stares at me now.

"Miss Thorne, I believe the thief known as the Leopard walked into this hotel this morning and stole your jewelry. I think he did it because he knew he could. I think he did it for his usual reasons—"

"Which are?" She interrupts me but doesn't appear startled to hear that the most infamous jewel thief in the world has made off with her beloved pieces. I admire her for it, though it's not wise to feel anything but professional courtesy toward her. Her ability to stay calm under pressure reminds me of a soldier fully aware the bomb is about to drop.

"Notoriety." I cough and resist spitting bits of stray tobacco from my tongue as I look about for an ashtray. Hotels should have a surplus of them, but I can't seem to locate one. As I reach for my coffee cup, Ania says, "That cup is fine china. Over there. On the side table by the water pitcher."

"Oh, thanks." I tap ash into a crystalline shell-like receptacle that looks much too fancy to be an ashtray, then clear my throat.

"Notoriety,'" she prompts.

"And money, of course, though selling stolen goods these days with the new regulations on contraband has become much harder."

"I should think notoriety comes after the money," she remarks.

"Not with him. He craves the attention. You could say he revels in it. The leopard-print gloves are his personal marketing campaign."

"Was he wearing them…?" Her smile is tight. "By the look on your face, no."

I keep expecting her to fall apart. Start sobbing, implore me to find her jewels, no matter what. Instead, she becomes even more remote, as if she's containing everything she must be feeling, hoarding it deep inside.

"He wasn't," I say. "Which doesn't help your case."

"Why not?"

"Because criminals like him keep to an established pattern. They do things the same way because it works." I pause, thinking I should clarify, though her expression indicates she understands. "Until it doesn't."

"Doesn't?" she repeats. Now, I hear a slight seam in her voice.

"Well, this note." I point to it on the table. "He's never written to one of his victims before. And the necklace. He's never returned anything he stole, either."

"But you still believe it's him?"

"He's the only one I know capable of doing this." I take another drag and crush my cigarette in the ashtray. "The note is deliberate. He wrote it to you personally."

"He took my list," she replies. "Sylvia told me. He knew for whom this necklace was intended, personally designed and designated by me."

"True. But he returned it in a very personalized way all the same." I pause once more to gauge her reaction. When I detect no signs of imminent breakdown, I add, "He targeted you for a reason. Beyond the value of your jewels. He's sending you a message."

"Sending it to me? Or to you?"

"What?" I feel myself recoil.

"Mr. Curtis." She smiles again. "Can we skip the pleasantries? I think you know I'm not a hysteric who needs protection from the harsh truth. And I can plainly see you're not nearly as uninvolved in this as you'd like me to think."

"Oh?" I make myself light another cigarette to disguise my discomfort.

"Yes. You have a stake here, too, beyond your responsibility to your employer. I know a stake when I see one. What is it?" Her eyes never leave mine, as if she can see into me, into the secrets stored in my inner vault. "Have you had dealings with this man before? Is that why you claim you're the only one for the job? Please. Don't lie or try to spare my feelings. Nothing you say could possibly upset me any more than I already am."

"I think you might be wrong about that," I tell her.

"Try me."

"Very well." My voice thickens. "Six years ago, he robbed a jewel cutter establishment in London at six-forty-five in the evening. This is confidential, but he took over a million sterling pounds in uncut diamonds. He shot the jewel cutter's assistant when she came upon him unexpectedly. I was on the case. I saw the mess she made, trying to keep him from taking the diamonds. I saw her body on the floor. She was thirty-two years old. Engaged to be married. It wasn't reported anywhere because I shut the press down. I've been on his trail ever since. A very dangerous man—a thief and a murderer—just sent you a note."

I see her swallow, watch the movement in the slim column of her throat.

"Miss Thorne, I think he changed his pattern because of that case. I think he's been waiting for the perfect opportunity to strike again. And he found it—in you."

"Are you saying…?" She draws in a breath. "He's after *me*?"

"Or something only you possess. He returned the necklace. From where I stand, his intent is clear: *it would be a crime*, he wrote. As if what he's already done isn't. But what he might do next will be."

She continues to hold my stare. Then I hear her say, "The pieces from our vault. They have significant value to my company."

"Yes." I wish I could do something to help her, as I see her grapple to take in what I'm implying. "You can't afford to take the risk. Not now."

She's instantly on her feet, moving to the white telephone in its cradle on the fancy gilded desk where she had her portfolio. She picks up the receiver. "*Bonjour.* Please, put me through to Miss Taylor's suite. Yes, I can hold." A few seconds go by, and I see her other hand curl into a fist on the desk. "Yes, please. Is my assistant Miss Morton there? Would you be so kind as to put her on the line? Thank you. Sylvia? Come here at once. No. Tell them I don't know about the replacements at this time. There's been an unexpected delay. I'm very sorry. No, Sylvia. I need you here. Now."

When she puts down the receiver, she turns to me. "I have to contact New York. The pieces are in transit. I told someone trustworthy on my staff to accompany them. They're due in Paris sometime this evening, but I don't know their precise arrival."

"Find out." I move to the suite doors. "I'll be back as soon as I can. I have to question the kitchen staff, try to find out how the necklace and note ended up on your salad plate."

As I open the doors, she calls out, "I want you to catch him, Mr. Curtis. I'll do whatever is necessary to help you catch him."

"I want to catch him, too," I say, but as I leave, I wonder which of us wants to catch him more.

And what he might do to evade us.

It doesn't surprise me that no one in the kitchen knows how it happened, but when I corner the waiter who made the delivery—one of the advantages of a five-star hotel is that they assign specific staff to high-paying clients—like clockwork, M. Saucey materializes. "M. Curtis, what's the meaning of this? You have no authority to question our employees."

I round on him. "A note and an item of extreme interest to my case was delivered to Miss Thorne with her room service. I want to know how it got there."

"I'm quite sure we bear no responsibility—"

I cut him off. "Shall we ask the gendarmes? Is that how you want to play this? Should we let them decide whose responsibility it is? Because someone in your kitchen put something that was definitely more than lettuce in Miss Thorne's salad. Let me assure you, if I get the police involved, your entire hotel will be under immediate investigation."

He speaks in rapid French to the waiter behind me, and though it's too staccato for me to decipher his words, I hear the demand in it anyway. The implicit threat.

The waiter is clutching a hand towel, wringing it into a knot. His reply is frightened.

"What did he say?" I bark at Saucey. I'm losing my short supply of patience.

Saucey, to his credit, looks astonished. I can tell it's not a common feeling for him. "He claims a mademoiselle interrupted him at the lift. She gave him the items in question and asked that he deliver them as instructed."

"A mademoiselle?" I eye the waiter. Young. No more than twenty or so. Looking like he's about to fall to his knees and cry. For what it's worth, I believe him. "Ask him what the mademoiselle looked like. Exactly what she said to him."

Saucey machine-guns the inquiry. The waiter has tears in his eyes as he answers.

"Well?" I ask Saucey.

"She was Miss Thorne's assistant. He recognized her. He delivered breakfast service to her earlier this morning before… He saw no reason to refuse her request." Saucey sniffs. "Regardless, he's no longer in our employ."

"Wait," I say as the waiter slumps in dejection. "You can't just fire him."

Saucey retorts, "I most certainly can. What he's done is against hotel policy."

"I don't give a rat's ass about your policy. Is he very sure the woman who gave him those items was Miss Thorne's assistant?"

"He is, Mr. Curtis. Entirely sure." Saucey draws himself to his full height in an effort to compensate for what's clearly been an intolerable breach of Carlton etiquette. It's wasted on me. I'm a good six inches taller than him in my bare feet. "I will apologize in person to Mademoiselle Thorne at once and assure her that nothing like this has ever occurred under my management—and shall never occur again."

"Forget it." I stride past him. "The last thing Miss Thorne needs is more of your service." I pause, shooting him a look. "And the waiter stays until I say so. Got it?"

I bound back to the lift. In the hallway to the suite, I have to take a moment to collect myself. I'm sweating like a hog under my jacket and can feel my shirt sticking to my chest, perspiration trickling down my nape into my collar. Loosening my tie, I run my fingers again through my damp hair, realize it's pointless, and proceed to the suite.

I hear her on the phone, speaking in French. Sylvia stands at the desk, packing papers and the portfolio into a briefcase. For a moment, I hesitate, thinking this has gone beyond my jurisdiction. I should call in the police. Make sure everyone involved is kept right where they are and wait for the Paris investigative team to arrive. This is a very serious situation that requires criminal experts. Professionals.

But I can't do it. Because I already know the Leopard is ahead of me. Because I know the experts are mired in bureaucracy that will slow everything to a crawl, to mounds of paperwork and signatures and authorizations required from above. Because no one is as professional as I am, even when I'm not. Because no one has my particular skills.

And he's finally within my grasp. I was wrong. He's not playing it safe this time. Safe is the last thing on his mind. And if he's not playing it safe, he can make another mistake.

"Miss Thorne." I lift my voice so she can hear me over whomever she's talking to on the phone. She glances over at me, annoyed. When she sees my expression, she says something into the phone and sets the receiver down.

"What is it?" she asks.

Sylvia stands frozen at the desk as I say, "I think Miss Morton needs to explain that."

"Explain?" Ania Thorne turns to her assistant in bewilderment. Her gaze darts from Sylvia's petrified face to mine and back again. "Will someone please *say* something?"

"She did it," I say. "Miss Morton gave him the codes to your cases."

"No!" Sylvia cries out.

Ania Thorne goes still. "That's…impossible."

"Is it?" I take a step toward Sylvia. "You delivered the necklace and the note. I just spoke to the service waiter. He recognized you. The thief told you to do it. Didn't he?"

Sylvia doesn't move. She's petrified in place. Then her mouth twitches. She's trying to contain herself, though it isn't until Ania Thorne says, "Is this true, Sylvia?" that she falls apart. I see it happen as if in slow motion, the way her hand hovers on the briefcase she was about to close, trembling. How her eyes turn wet, and her face crumples. Her hands come up to cover her mouth, stifling the sob that erupts past her fingers.

Ania Thorne makes an immediate move toward her.

"No." I put myself between her and the desk.

"She's my assistant. She's been in my employ for twelve years," Ania hisses at me. "And I'm telling you, it's simply *not* possible."

"Sylvia," I say. She lets out another sob, tears streaming down her cheeks. "Why?"

"He…" This time, I think I'm not wrong in assuming a woman is about to faint. She sways at the desk. "Get her some water," I tell Ania, who hastens to a pitcher on the side table. When she starts to hand the glass to Sylvia, I take it from her. Ania's fingers are icy.

"Let me handle this, okay?" I say. Ania Thorne clenches her jaw but retreats to the sofa. I set the glass on the desk. "Drink it. Take your time."

Sylvia gulps down half the glass and stands dazed as if hit by a mallet before whispering, "He threatened John."

"Darcy?" I clarify.

"Yes." She wipes at her eyes, streaking her mascara. She looks only at me, avoiding her employer on the sofa. "He—he told me that John… He knew…things about him. Things that would ruin him and reflect badly on Ania for hiring him. Oh, God."

"Take your time," I say again. I let a few seconds pass. "How did he do it? In person?"

"No." She shakes her head. "Not in person. It happened so fast. So unexpectedly."

"This morning?" I ask skeptically.

"In Paris, shortly after we arrived." She jerks around the desk toward Ania, but I block her. "I didn't want to harm you," she says, her voice fracturing. "Ania, I swear it. I would die before I ever hurt you. You know that. I never meant for any of this to—"

"To me." My voice wrenches her gaze back to my face. "Talk to me, Miss Morton."

She nods convulsively. Guilt is an awful burden to carry and a powerful incentive. Some of the cases I've investigated got solved because of it. An envious sibling. A thwarted lover. A vengeful rival. Sometimes, art and jewels aren't stolen by strangers but by those closest to the victim, for the most banal reasons.

The worst happens because no one ever thinks it can.

"Paris," I say. "What happened there?"

"We landed at Orly. Ania—Miss Thorne—she was tired, so we took the car to her residence. We were leaving for Cannes early the next day, and she had several important phone calls to make. Mr. Darcy took the cases to the bank vault."

I glance over my shoulder at Ania. She gives a terse nod. "I never keep jewels in my homes. The company maintains international bank vaults in cities for when I travel, especially when we don't have a safe in our stores. Our Paris boutique doesn't have a safe strong enough for what I was bringing to the festival, so we used the bank instead."

I return to Sylvia. "Go on."

"We had appointments to confirm." She glances frantically past me to Ania. "We had to see which clients had already arrived in Cannes, whose schedules had changed. It was a very busy late afternoon for us after a long day of travel, so I didn't notice until the evening when Miss Thorne called for her car to go out for dinner that John hadn't returned."

"Is that unusual?" I ask.

Ania cuts in, "Mr. Darcy is my security detail. He took the cases to the vault, and I told him to get some rest afterwards. He's not my chauffeur. I don't need security to dine at Maxim's. I assume he went to rest, as instructed."

"So?" I say to Sylvia. "What then?"

"Ania left for dinner. I tidied up in the flat and went to John's hotel."

"Darcy doesn't stay in your Paris flat?" I ask Ania.

She gives me a look. "It's Paris. Two bedrooms. The hotel I book for John is just down the street from my residence. Not far."

The wealthy rely too little on common sense.

"Was John at the hotel?"

Sylvia pulls a handkerchief from her skirt pocket to dab her eyes.

"Yes. He was very disturbed. He told me that as he left the bank, a car pulled up to the curb, and he heard his name. He thought it was Ania, though it wasn't her car—the Peugeot we use in Paris. When he approached, the window slid down a crack—he said the glass was tinted—and a man he didn't know said…" Her voice falters. She casts an imploring gaze at Ania. "We should have told you. I begged John to tell you, but he was so worried for his job—"

"Miss Morton. What did the man say?"

"He knew things. About the war. What John did. John wouldn't explain to me. I don't know what he did. He's never mentioned it before. But I could see he was agitated. Very concerned. For himself. For Ania. The man threatened to expose him for something right before the festival that would create terrible press for the company."

My blood chills in my veins. I feel it creep through me, icing my sweat-drenched shirt under my jacket. I focus on maintaining my expression, to not reveal for an instant that I know exactly what John was so concerned about.

"What did this stranger in the car want in exchange?"

"The codes to the cases," whispers Sylvia, and when Ania lets out a furious gasp, Sylvia says desperately, "John didn't have them! He never has them."

"But you did," I say.

I hear the silken rustle of Ania's skirt as she rises abruptly to her feet. "Enough." Her voice is a blade. "Sylvia didn't know the codes, either. Only I know them. They're devised in-house by my accountant and programmed directly into the case locks. I never give anyone access to the codes. Never."

"Do you write them down?" I turn to her. Her face is glacial. But under her mask, I can see she's stunned. It's always like this. When the truth slips out, and it's someone they trust, it hurts more than anything they could have imagined.

"Yes, of course. But I destroyed the paper as soon as I memorized them…" She lifts a hand to her throat. "Sylvia, please. Tell me this isn't true."

Sylvia Morton looks down at her feet and starts to weep like a child.

"You gave the paper to Sylvia to destroy," I say to Ania, who steps back. Just a small step, but I see a lifetime of trust and devotion dissolve in that one movement. Severed.

Ania turns away, folding her arms about herself. "You have to understand. Events like the festival…it's insane the last few days before we depart—a million things to take care of, a million last-minute details requiring my attention. The codes aren't programmed into the cases until the night before we leave, after I've seen the jewels packed. I didn't think." She draws in a tight breath, and I see her shoulder blades make a sharp indent under her taut grey jacket. "I didn't think," she repeats.

I turn back to Sylvia. "Did you tell John what you were going to do?"

She can barely speak now. "He would never have allowed it. He didn't know."

"What about the necklace and note?"

She makes a sound of despair.

"He gave them to you during the heist," I say. "He told you what to do with them."

Sylvia can't bring herself to admit it, but I see the truth in her eyes. They can never hide the guilt from their eyes, if they have any remorse.

"Well." I pull out a cigarette, light it.

"*Well?*" Ania bursts out. I'm actually relieved to hear it, the rage cracking her impermeable façade, tinting her alabaster cheeks with color and darkening her storm-colored gaze. She needs to feel it. She needs to feel and accept it.

"We now know how he did it," I say. She stares at me as if she wants to hit me. I would let her if I thought it would help. But I know she wants to hit herself more. That, too, she must feel. As long as she doesn't wallow in it for too long.

Much as I don't like to admit it, I need her more than ever.

"He threatened a member of your staff to get to you," I go on, thinking she needs concrete facts to hold onto. "So, Miss Morton took it upon herself to protect both of you. You did know Darcy and Miss Morton are…?"

An acidic laugh escapes her. "Mr. Curtis, I'm not blind. I don't forbid my employees from falling in love, as long as it doesn't interfere with the business. Until now, it hasn't."

"It's my fault," Sylvia says. "I'm sorry. I'm so sorry. I never meant it. I never…"

"There was no money exchanged. No bribery," I tell Ania as I take in her anguished expression, her struggle to reconcile herself to what she's learned. "He used blackmail. He knew how the bad press would reflect on you if whatever he knew about Darcy got out. He knew where the weakness was and precisely how and when to strike."

"He certainly did, didn't he?" She shifts her gaze from Sylvia to me. "But I believe Mr. Darcy is an acquaintance of yours from the war, isn't he? What could you and John Darcy have possibly done to lead my assistant to betray me and allow the Leopard to steal my jewels?"

Chapter Four

Ania

"What Darcy or I did isn't the point. It won't solve our problems," says Mr. Curtis, his voice going tense.

His response angers me, especially knowing what I do. "I beg to differ. If it weren't for whatever happened, I'd not be here with my business collapsing about me—"

He interrupts. "Miss Thorne, if you trust nothing else, trust me when I say that what happened was the result of the war, a tragedy of unimaginable magnitude. John Darcy is a hero. I know you're upset, and I don't blame you. But explaining what happened ten years ago won't help us get your jewels back or prevent the Leopard from striking again."

Is he actually *lecturing* me? For a moment, my rage boils to the surface, but then I realize, given the grim look on his face, whatever happened isn't something he's put behind him. He keeps secrets—like we all do. Though he may think I've no right to pry into his past—even though it affects me now—I should have a care. He's the only person who can help me. Putting us at odds won't serve my interests.

"Very well," I say. "I apologize if I overstepped."

He looks surprised. He nods and gives me a pained smile. Jerome Curtis has a hard-won smile. It doesn't light up his face. Rather it seems to hurt for him to move his muscles in that way. I've met other men torn apart by the war, those who somehow managed to patch themselves back together. They're never easy to be with. Never whole again. This man has clearly been through hell and survived it. For now, the least I can do is respect that.

But I'm not going to forget what I've discovered.

"So, what do you suggest we do?" I ask.

"Get to Paris as soon as we can to protect your shipment. Whoever is behind this could be planning to steal the replacements. And seeing as he managed to do the impossible here—I wouldn't put anything past him."

"Leave?" I say. "Now? With the festival about to open and the most important stars in the world awaiting those replacements from me?"

"I thought we decided that. I thought we agreed you can't risk what might happen if we're not there to take charge of the jewelry when it arrives in Paris."

My brief empathy toward him evaporates. I want to throw him out, enraged by his self-assurance, as if I have no say in the very matter overturning my existence.

"You don't understand," I inform him. "If I fail to deliver the replacements as promised, I stand to lose not only some of my most valued clientele but also my reputation. Who will trust me again if I can't make good on my promises?"

He rubs his chin, regarding me as if I'm a spoiled brat. "Miss Thorne, I get it. I really do. But if those pieces end up in the Leopard's hands, you'll have nothing left to repair. No company, either. No insurance firm on this planet will cover you again, so you can say goodbye to your valued clientele and your endangered reputation."

Damn him. He's right. In my mind's eye, I see the leather cases with the historical pieces taken from our vault, iconic pieces that cemented my father's place in the annals of jewelry fame. Should something happen to them, I'll have sacrificed his legacy, turned my back on our heritage and, yes, effectively bankrupted the company. We can't possibly overcome another loss of such magnitude.

"I'm sure a dozen other jewelers can satisfy the stars for the festival," he adds with that infuriating nonchalance of his. "Let's go to Paris to meet that plane."

It would be a crime...

"And what do you propose I do about my appointments here?" I hear the arrogance in my voice, disguising my uncertainty. It appalls me. How have I been reduced to such a pathetic state, unable to prioritize my responsibilities? The future of my company is at risk.

He looks at Sylvia, still standing by the desk, her face lowered.

"No," I say at once. "I'm not leaving her in charge." Sylvia flinches at my harsh pronouncement, and it hurts me to see it, but she's gone too far for forgiveness. However well-intended her motives might have been, she helped put me in this awful position.

He shrugs. "She can't do any harm. No jewels are left here to steal. No one to blackmail. Why not let her manage the appointments and keep your clients cooling their heels? At least until we've secured the replacements. If we don't..." A frown crosses his brow.

"Yes?" I say, dreading his answer.

He shakes his head. "Let's take this one step at a time, okay? I'll call the airport in Nice and see if I can arrange a plane to—"

"I have a plane. At the Cannes-Mandelieu airport."

"A private aircraft." He gives me a wry look. "Right. Of course, you do."

I decide not to dignify his sarcasm with a reply. Despite it, he looks relieved. Even with the tension between us, it makes me want to smile. You can take the boy out of the working class, but you can't take the working class out of the boy.

"I can call ahead to have the plane readied," Sylvia offers. "Please, Ania. Let me help."

"I'll call." I want to rely on her as little as possible, though I haven't made a decision as to what I should do. Logic dictates I turn her over to the police. She gave the thief my codes. But she's also been my devoted assistant for twelve years—and, I now realize belatedly, an unacknowledged friend. Until now, I had no cause to doubt her. And though I don't like to admit it, I never once asked about her involvement with Darcy. I knew, of course, but I never said a word. I behaved as if it didn't exist because it made me envious because Sylvia had found a life beyond work, a fulfillment I've never had.

"See if they can do it fast," Mr. Curtis tells me. "Have you called New York yet to find out when the other plane is expected to land?"

"I will," I say, though the last thing I want to do is make more calls. I'm not ready to concede defeat. But I don't have a choice anymore. I've lost my bearings, my compass. With Sylvia exposed, Darcy a liability, and hundreds of thousands of dollars of jewels missing—a scandal soon to be reported in every newspaper across the world—I'm on my own, with nowhere to turn, and no one to trust. No one, except this stranger in his creased gaberdine suit with his all-too-keen eyes.

Should I even trust him, knowing he and Darcy did something so terrible it was blackmail fodder?

"I must call my father, too," I say impulsively. It makes me feel more in control to state a decision not imposed by others. No matter what's happened in the past, no matter how ruinous his decisions may have been, Papa has been my touchstone. I'm still his daughter, no matter what. I don't know why I feel the need to assert myself to Mr. Curtis, and from his reluctant assent, I can see he doesn't either. But he doesn't protest. It's not his business, and he knows it. And while I appreciate it, I also can't stand it.

"And you don't have to treat me like I'm made of glass," I tell him. "I don't break easily. I have diamond dust in my blood. And the only thing that can cut a diamond is another diamond."

That odd expression surfaces again in his eyes as if I've just given him a clue to some unfathomable puzzle. "While you make your calls, I'll go speak to Darcy."

I march into the bedroom. As I dial the phone, I find my hand shaking. My father's butler answers. Gerard has been with my family since before I was born, and hearing his voice brings sudden tears to my eyes. I have an instant longing to be nineteen years old again, living in my father's luxurious duplex on 64th Street and working at Cartier. Coming home every night brimming with design ideas and sitting with Papa to tell him about it. When Thorne & Company was thriving, and my father was the most lauded jeweler in the United States, treated like royalty everywhere he went. Now, he's practically a recluse. An outcast. And I fear I might be fast on my way to becoming one, too.

"Ania. Such a lovely surprise," Gerard says. "It's been far too long, hasn't it?"

He always calls me by my first name. Until I turned eighteen, and he started referring to me as Miss Thorne. I hated it and refused to respond. After a month-long statement, he relented and reverted to Ania.

"Gerard." I curb the falter in my voice. "I need to talk to Papa."

"I'm so sorry. Mr. Thorne isn't here at present. He left for Europe a week ago."

"Europe?" I say, bewildered. My father is on the same continent as me and never thought to tell me? It reinforces my discomfort, my painful realization that we've grown apart over the past six years. It wasn't my decision to see him ousted by our board. I never wanted to be the company director. But the board insisted it was the only way we could continue to operate. I was the imagination behind the collections, and the clients might still trust me. While Papa's last lawsuit, for which the client countersued for a million dollars, had resulted in major outrage and headlines. His inability to be diplomatic and rely on the board rather than himself to resolve differences had cost us too much. He'd said he understood. The time had come for him to retire. Before the company's well-being, nothing else mattered. He agreed to leave and support my appointment as the new director. If he had to be replaced, who better than his daughter, whom he'd trained to follow in his footsteps?

"He was invited to the opening of Sir Michael Brigham's new musical in London," Gerard explains, "and then I believe he's going to spend some time in Barcelona. There's a new Picasso exhibit there. You know how much he loves modern art."

"Yes, I do," I say. Jewels, art, music: my father's triptych of passions. Michael Brigham used to be a penniless composer in New York, working on off-Broadway productions when he met my aunt Agnes, a starlet in motion pictures. They fell in love and married, making my father the benevolent brother-in-law. He knew everyone in the theater world and invited them to a soiree in our apartment to hear Michael's original score. After that, everything fell into place. Twenty-five years later, Michael is a knight anointed by the Queen, with touring companies worldwide performing his popular musicals.

"Do you require the telephone number in London, Ania?" Gerard asks. "He's staying with Sir Michael and Lady Agnes at their home."

"No, I have their number. Thank you, Gerard."

"Anytime, Ania. Please don't be a stranger. We miss you here."

"I miss you, too," I whisper and hang up before I start crying.

I dial my uncle Michael's London residence. The maid who answers the phone relays that neither my father nor my uncle is in, but that I can leave a message. I start to give one until I realize I'll have to explain the situation to a servant, when news of the theft hasn't yet been reported. My father won't be able to contact me anyway while I'm in transit to Paris, so I say I'll call back. Then I contact the airport to have my plane readied and finally call New York again to ensure the information I received previously remains the same.

Jerome Curtis and I are very quiet on our way to the airport. Normally, it's a ten-minute drive, but the festival has created traffic worthy of Manhattan at rush hour. By the time we reach the airport and board my plane, an hour has passed. I can see Curtis is anxious. He keeps reaching into his pocket to fidget with his lighter. He probably wants to smoke, but it's not allowed aboard the plane. My rule. The flight time from Cannes to Paris takes little more than two hours. It's now two-thirty in the afternoon. The jewels are supposed to arrive in Paris at approximately eight p.m., so we have plenty of time. If everything goes according to schedule, we'll arrive with more than two hours to spare.

But, of course, nothing goes according to plan. Our plane can't take off because of sudden winds. We're delayed on the tarmac for forty minutes, with Jerome pacing back and forth, his tall frame crammed into the plane's interior until my steward informs him that pursuant to regulations, he must remain seated with his seat belt fastened. Mr. Curtis scowls but returns to his seat, though the same winds slow us down once we depart, lengthening our flight to three hours.

"I thought rich people flew privately for convenience," he remarks sourly as we touch down in Le Bourget Airport.

"Mr. Curtis," I retort, "not even the rich can control the weather. We're an hour's drive to Orly. We will make it in time."

"I hope so." He uncoils his lean body from the seat. "By the way, why don't you call me Jerome? I think we're past the *Mr. Curtis* stage, don't you?"

"Do you expect to call me by my first name, too?" I eye him as he runs a hand through his hair. It's practically standing up in thick spikes. Doesn't he keep a comb on his person? He boarded the plane with a leather satchel that would barely hold my cosmetics. He saw me staring at it and chuckled—that irritating dry chuckle of his—and said he prefers to travel light.

"No," he now replies to my question. "I never expect anything. I find life's easier that way."

"Fine. Call me Ania." As I turn to retrieve my overnight bag from the steward, Jerome says, "Before we go to your car, have Mr. Regulations here radio Orly to keep your staff and the cases on the plane until we get there. Tell them not to let anyone else on board but us."

I take a deep breath and nod, trying to remain as calm as I can. I'm not used to this kind of crisis, even less to being told what to do. No one has told me how to behave since I became the company director, except the board, and they've never had to instruct me because I witnessed enough of my father's misbehavior to know what not to do. To be ordered about by someone I regard as a hired gun from an outside insurance firm, with whom I've had no prior dealings, grates on my already raw nerves.

I'm not as prepared as I thought I was. Tell me someone needs a piece of jewelry for a gala, and no one is more competent. That's my arena, my expertise. I can assess the client, know what she desires and how long it will take to deliver it. But winds and traffic and roadways—I'm at their mercy. And being ordered around by a man I barely know? It all makes me want to shout in helpless fury.

To my relief—and no doubt his—the airport allows my car to drive onto the tarmac to meet us so there are no further delays to gripe about.

We reach Orly in time, boarding the company plane to find Luke Westerly from my office. He's my second-in-command when I'm not there, not co-director, but a longtime trusted employee, who also worked under my father and knows our company inside and out. A handsome, silvering man of a certain age, always impeccable in three-piece tailored suits from Saville Row and English lavender cologne. A lifelong bachelor, too, devoted to Thorne & Company, which is why I insisted that he accompany the cases from New York.

"We had a bit of excitement while we were waiting for you," Luke says.

"Oh?" Beside Luke, who's dapper as ever despite the ten-hour trip, Jerome Curtis looks as if he rolled out of bed and grabbed whatever he found strewn on the floor.

Luke gives him a cursory glance before he says to me, "Once we landed, a member of the ground crew came aboard to report they'd spotted smoke coming from our tail. He insisted we must de-plane immediately."

I feel my heart start to pound. "The cases?"

"We wanted to take them with us. I demanded, in fact, but the crewmember insisted we leave all our belongings on the plane. Given what's happened, I argued with him rather strenuously. As it turned out, there wasn't anything to be concerned about—"

"This man," interrupts Jerome, "what did he say once you disembarked, and no problem was found with the plane?"

"Nothing." Luke turns his curious gaze to Jerome. "He left."

"He *left?*" Jerome's voice rises in sudden anger. As Luke blinks—like me, he's not accustomed to being on the receiving end of that tone of voice from anyone, much less a disheveled stranger—I say urgently, "Where are the cases now?"

Luke gestures to the rear compartment. "Exactly where I left them."

As I feel my entire body sag in relief, Jerome growls at Luke. "Can you describe him?"

"Not well, I'm afraid." Luke glances at me. I nod. "He was in some sort of baggy uniform, the way all ground crew seem to dress these days. A cap. Glasses. I didn't pay much attention when he first came on board, other than to think he was dressed rather shabbily for a customs official, which is what I initially thought he was. I certainly didn't pay more attention other than to try and understand what he was saying."

"Understand? Don't you speak French?"

Luke regards Jerome in amusement. "I am fluent in French. He was the one who spoke very poor English. I answered him in French, but he seemed intent on conducting our entire conversation in English. Excuse me, but may I ask who you are, Mr...?"

"Curtis. How tall was he?"

"I suppose about my height. Five feet eleven or so," Luke says.

"So little more than average. What about hair color? Approximate age?"

"I'd say his hair was brown, but his cap hid it. It was a rather large cap. As for his age, maybe forty or so? As I said, I didn't pay much attention to his appearance. We'd just landed and were informed of a possible fire on board. It was precipitous, as you can imagine."

"Are you telling me nothing about this man struck you as strange?"

"I found the entire situation strange," replies Luke.

Despite Jerome's barrage of questions, I want to think there's no reason to suspect anything nefarious. No reason other than suspicion, after hours of suspicion. No reason, other than things I never thought possible already happening—like betrayal by someone close to me and the theft of my jewelry.

"So, he was never alone with the cases?" Jerome asks.

"Well, he did insist on escorting us off the plane, but the cases were in the compartment, and only I have the key. Besides the short time during which I assume he inspected the plane's interior, I've been with the cases the entire time."

"Let's just get them into the car," I say, preempting another acerbic comment from Jerome. I can tell he doesn't understand Luke's evident disdain, and Luke is likewise baffled to find me with a man completely unknown to him.

With Luke's assistance, we load the four cases into the car. My driver, Henri, steers us from the airport toward the city and the 6th arrondissement, where my residence is located on Rue de Université. Though it hasn't been stated aloud, I assume both men will stay with me. I have a second bedroom, and they can share it or take turns staying up all night if need be until we—

From the front seat, Jerome suddenly says, "Someone's following us."

Luke leans across the back seat to whisper in my ear, "Ania, darling. I don't mean to be rude, but *who* exactly is this person?"

Before his words can register, Jerome turns to me. "Look out the rear window. The black Mercedes. It's been trailing us for the last ten minutes." As I crane my head to peer out, Jerome orders my driver, "Take a detour. Now. Lose that car."

"Whatever is going on?" Luke exclaims.

"Luke," I hiss at him. "Not now."

Jerome is staring into the side-view mirror as Henri abruptly swerves into a labyrinth of narrow side streets—a lifelong Parisian, he knows this city intimately. Within minutes, I hear Jerome sigh. "Good. It's no longer behind us."

"Are you sure?" I say. My voice is ragged. "Jerome? Are you sure?"

He doesn't answer, leaning to Henri. "Any hotels nearby? With separate entrances?"

"*Bien-sur*," says Henri. "The Ritz. On Place Vendome and on Rue Cambon."

"Go there." Jerome turns again to me. "We'll check in. Leave the cases with your associate and exit by the second entrance to hail a cab. Your driver will proceed to your residence without us while we find another hotel."

"Another hotel? Why? My residence is perfectly—" I cut myself short. I was about to say my residence is perfectly safe, but no place feels safe anymore.

"Because your plane wasn't inspected for fire when it landed at Orly. It was being examined, probably to ascertain if the cases were on board. He knows they're here, and he's expecting us to take the cases to your residence. We have to divide to confuse him."

"But how can we just leave the cases in the Ritz with Luke?" I protest as Henri pulls up to the fabled hotel. "We don't even know if they have a vault secure enough to—"

"Listen to me," Jerome says. "I have a plan. Not much of one, I'll admit, but it might work if you do as I say. We're going to set a trap."

Luke mumbles under his breath, "This all sounds very illicit."

"More than you know," I say, returning Jerome's stare. "Leopards don't like to be trapped."

"They don't. But only a trap will catch him."

Chapter Five

Jerome

After we board Ania's private plane—and let me say, privilege may lead to poor judgment, but at least you can suffer it in a flying suite with a full bar—and she pulls out documents from an overnight bag that would satisfy my requirements for two weeks, I lean back in the upholstered seat, loosen my seat belt, and gaze out the rounded window onto banks of foamy white clouds.

I should get some sleep. I can survive on none when needed, but the turmoil since my arrival in Cannes has earned me some well-deserved shut-eye. Yet even when I resolutely close my eyes—as much to avoid watching her beautiful, determined face as she peruses those documents as to invoke a brief oblivion I already know won't come—I think of Darcy and the anguish on his face when I found him in his room, nursing his headache after having been examined by the hotel doctor.

All I had to do was knock on his door. He took one look at me and groaned.

"Sylvia told you."

I stepped into his room. "She had no choice." I explained what happened, and when his eyes widened— "That bastard actually sent *a note* with the necklace?"—I informed him how I also discovered he'd been accosted and blackmailed in Paris.

"That's why you thought it was the Leopard from the start, wasn't it?" I said. "You suspected it from the moment he pulled up in that car outside the bank."

"No." Darcy squared his shoulders and turned to the side table by the bed and a half-empty bottle of Jack Daniels. "I didn't think it was the Leopard then. I thought it was some creep trying to intimidate me into scaring Miss Thorne from attending the festival." He poured himself a glass and gulped it down. "I didn't think he'd steal anything."

"John, getting soused isn't going to help. We have a very serious problem here that we both need to deal with."

"We?" He gave a coarse laugh. "That's rich, coming from you. How is it your problem? Looks to me, you have a cushy job working for an insurance firm, investigating high-rolling heists. I have—or I *had*—a job with a fine jewelry company that's just taken a huge hit because of what I did."

"What we did," I said quietly. "I was there, too. Remember?"

"Yeah. I remember, all right." He reached for the bottle again, then thought better of it and slumped onto the bed, clasping his big hands between his thighs as he stared at the floor. "I wish I didn't. I wish it never happened. Fucking Nazis. Fucking war. Fucked me up."

"I know." I felt awkward. We were friends once. Well, if not friends, then close enough. Because in war, friendship is a luxury that's less important than loyalty to your fellow soldier. It's life or death, not happy hour at the bar after a bad day at work. In war, it's never happy hour. It's always a bad day at work. "I wish it never happened, too. But it did. We both knew what the consequences might be."

"Did we?" He lifted his bloodshot eyes. "I mean, really know?"

"We did. That's why I agreed to keep it secret. John, I never broke my promise to you."

He reached for the bottle then, drank right out of it.

"How did this happen? How did he manage to find out and use it against you?"

Darcy cradled the bottle as if considering draining it. Then he said in a voice that made a crack in my heart, "I told them. When our unit was discharged, I made a full disclosure."

"What?" I suddenly couldn't move. "You *told* them?"

"I did." He reared his head again. "I couldn't live with it. I couldn't stand myself. I wasn't sleeping. I was drinking too much. I was having nightmares all the time, even when I was awake. It was eating me up inside."

I swallowed. I knew what he described, Not the drinking as I'd always avoided that pitfall, but the rest… I knew the rest. All of us had experienced it to one degree or another: every soldier on the front lines who reached Poland. And later, after Berlin fell, when we signed up to avenge what we'd seen.

Some things, you never forgot.

"Who did you tell?" I asked.

"The brass. Who else? They interviewed all of us before we were discharged, remember? To see who was fit for service in another section, and who was fit to be kicked into the streets. I qualified for the second option. I made sure of it. I was ashamed, Jerome." His fingers clenched around the bottle. "Ashamed of myself. I didn't deserve a transfer. Hell, as far as I was concerned, I didn't deserve honorable discharge, either."

"But you got one. We both did." It was starting to make sense, the reason I'd also found myself out in the cold after years of dedicated service as a soldier and covert operative. I'd never understood it. I figured they wanted to shut it down and pretend it never existed. Best way to do that was to quietly re-assign or dismiss those of us who knew.

"Yeah, we both got one," muttered Darcy.

"Did you name me in your report?"

He went quiet, not looking at me.

"John. Did you name me?"

"I told them everything. I guess that means I named you."

"So, they knew about the night in Dessau."

He took a swig from the bottle. "Don't worry. I said I told them everything. How you tried to stop me, and I refused to listen. How we'd been up for nearly six days straight, tracking that sonofabitch, and I lost it when we finally got to him. I put it all on me, okay? It was on me. I beat him to death in that basement. Not you."

"John." I forced myself to take a step toward him. "I helped you cover it up. I was your commanding officer. We claimed on the incident report that he'd committed suicide before we found him, and we buried the body because it was already decaying. That makes me an accomplice. It makes me as guilty as you think you are."

"I am guilty!" He flung the bottle across the room. As it smashed against the wall, he panted, "For God's sake, I beat him to death with my fists."

"You killed a man who slaughtered women, children, the elderly—"

"He didn't kill them." John staggered to his feet. Despite his size, he looked so small in that moment. So broken. "He was a bureaucrat. He wasn't one of those butchers in the camps. He didn't pour the gas. He sat at a desk in an office and he…"

His voice faded, catching in his throat, as I said, "Drew up the lists for deportations to Auschwitz and Treblinka. He was responsible for emptying the Warsaw ghetto of whoever was left after the insurrection." I heard my voice harden. "John, what we did…you have to forgive yourself. You lost control. So did they. They lost control of their humanity. Their morality. Their goddamn decency. They murdered over six million Jews, John. People who did nothing to deserve it."

"I was a soldier." Tears thickened his voice. "I wasn't one of them. I enlisted because I wanted to defeat them. But that night in Dessau—God help me, I was no better than them. I murdered a scared old man in cold blood."

I made a move to touch him. I felt as if I had to do something, but he wrenched away from me, treading in his socks over the shards of the bottle scattered across the carpet.

"I got what was coming to me. The moment that car pulled up to the curb outside the bank, and he told me, I knew. Here it is, Darcy. Your payback."

I had my answer. He'd made an official disclosure, refuting what we'd reported. And he was right; we had murdered an old man in a bombed-out basement—a low-level bureaucrat, who worked in an office in Warsaw like hundreds of other bureaucrats in hundreds of other offices set up to industrialize an industry of mass-murder.

Somehow, Darcy's disclosure had been leaked to the thief I believe is the Leopard. Which means he knows I was involved and must have me in his sights, too. What he used against Darcy could be used against me.

It could cost me everything.

"Mr. Curtis? Mr. Curtis, are you awake?"

My eyes snap open to find Ania Thorne staring at me over her papers. "Are you hungry? We can have lunch served. The steward just informed me the flight is going to take longer than expected. Heavy winds, I'm afraid."

And now, here we are. Outside the Ritz Hotel, a bastion of the rich and famous like its tit-domed sister in Cannes. Ania looks wild-eyed and pale as we deal with the solicitous inquiry of the doorman, the gracious offer to take our luggage to reception and our less-than-gracious refusal, then the ordeal at reception itself, the immediate recognition—"Mademoiselle Thorne, an honor. Yes, we have a room available. Of course, it's no imposition. A reservation isn't required as we're not fully booked. For one? Certainly. Right this way, *s'il vous plaît*"—then the walk that seems to take forever to the elevators, past glamorous people in the glamorous lobby preparing to do glamorous things in glamorous Paris. The ride to the fifth floor, accompanied by a uniformed porter who's not allowed to actually carry anything but Mr. Cologne's monogrammed suitcase, filled no doubt with those expensive well-fitted suits he appears to wear like armor. The reverential unlocking of the hotel room door, the obligatory tour of the luxurious facilities, the generous tip, and finally, the porter's ceremonious departure, leaving us alone.

I set the two cases I'm carrying on the bed, which for a single is big enough to accommodate three of me. Mr. Cologne places the other two cases beside them as Ania steps into the bathroom. Mr. Cologne then unbuttons his cashmere overcoat, hangs it in the closet, and turns to me with an arched eyebrow as if I might taint the air with my breath.

"Mr. Curtis, perhaps you'd now care to tell me what all the subterfuge is about?"

I don't like the guy. He's one of those sophisticated, always-perfectly-dressed and pompous asses who make me feel as if I'm a smudge on their two-tone shoes.

"I don't answer to you," I tell him and enjoy the way he blinks. Guess he's never been in the army and refused what's not his business to hear.

"Luke, please." Ania emerges from the bathroom. She's freshened up, put on lipstick, and adjusted her hair, tightening the knot at her nape so her eyes appear very large and luminous, her cheekbones hollowed. She needs a decent meal. Gorgeous, but too thin, as if she's never enjoyed a greasy burger and fries, only those little salads with white chicken, croutons, and crumbs of goat cheese. With necklaces.

"Tell me instead," she says, turning to me. "What is your plan?"

"Open the cases," I reply.

I see her hesitate. It hurts me. I'm taken aback by the sudden knot it lodges in my chest. I know she's seen the gun under my jacket, so I remove it and fling it onto the bed beside the cases, then unbuckle the holster and toss it there, too. "Just to reassure you. If there's any doubt, Mr. Cologne here can take my gun and aim at me the entire time." I glance at him. "Do you know how to aim a gun?"

"The name is Luke Westerly." To his credit, he laughs. "You're not the sort of gentleman one is accustomed to." He extracts a key from an inner pocket of his vest. "Ania?"

She nods, still hesitant. I think she must know how to aim a gun.

He unlocks the cases and unfolds them like leathery petals to reveal the concave, cushioned interiors. The jewels nested there like glittering eggs. Dazzling. Leaping to fiery life even in the subdued light of the room. Pendants. Bracelets. Diadems. I recognize the different types of pieces and a few of the stones. I have to know at least the basics to be able to itemize and estimate the cost of the stolen goods I investigate, though I usually only see them in photographs after they've gone missing. Like I said, I'm no connoisseur, but you don't need to be one to know this is quite the haul.

"Wow."

Ania reaches over to caress a particularly large sea-green emerald in an ornate diamond-studded centerpiece. "My father made this out of a Romanov tiara," she says softly. "He acquired it at auction from a collection belonging to the late Duchess of Windsor. He re-cut the stone himself because part of it was chipped. The tiara was in very bad shape after years of neglect, but this stone…" Her fingertips pass over it as if it's made of delicate skin. "A grand duchess wore it. We don't know its complete history, only that it was cataloged in the Imperial Collection and smuggled out of Russia during the Revolution, after which it went through several hands before the duchess acquired it."

She looks at me. "Everything you see. This emerald choker. The sapphire parure. The yellow diamond suite. My father's most iconic pieces, worn by the heiress Barbara Hutton. By Greta Garbo. Marlene Dietrich. Each piece is nearly priceless now, not just because stones like these are increasingly hard to obtain, but for their historic value."

"Impressive," I say.

Luke laughs again. "Under that gruff exterior, I believe you might have the soul of a poet, Mr. Curtis. Impressive, indeed."

I glare at him. He smiles back. The man certainly knows how to hold his own. "Put all of the pieces into your bag," I tell her.

"You can't be serious." Ania stares at me. "The cases are designed to hold these pieces. I can't just pile the jewels on top of my belongings."

"Only a diamond can cut another diamond," I quote, and her face darkens. "Leave whatever you brought that won't fit in the bag. Do it quickly. We lost him for now, but it won't be for long. He's looking for us. He'll figure it out. We need to be out of here before he does."

As she upends her overnight bag, spilling out too many skirts, blouses, trousers, shoes, and stockings, with unsettling glimpses of black lace lingerie, and then starts extracting the pieces from the cases to wrap them in her plethora of scarves, I turn to Luke Westerly.

"After we leave, wait for an hour or so, then ring downstairs and inform the manager you wish to make arrangements for tomorrow to take the cases to the bank. Then wait for us to contact you. Don't let the cases out of your sight. It has to look real."

"Very well." He adjusts his necktie. "May I assume this could entail putting myself at risk? I'm no fool, Mr. Curtis. It's obvious the thief you think stole from us in Cannes is here in Paris. And from what I'm gathering, he plans to make another spectacular heist."

"You catch on fast. Are you up to it?"

"Believe me, I can aim that pistol if I must. And shoot it."

"I'm taking my gun." I strap the holster back on. "But I'm glad to hear it."

"Not all the jewels fit." Ania heaves an exasperated breath. "I can leave some of my shoes here, but I need my clothes. I told you—"

"Ania, my sweet. You're upset. Let me." Luke Westerly expertly bundles up the remaining pieces in her lingerie and tucks them into the crevices of her bag, flattening her bulging bag of cosmetics—why must women carry so much makeup?—over the top and zipping her bag shut. "There, tucked in like children." He gestures to the various pairs of high heels left on the bed. "I'll guard these with my life, darling. Don't you fret."

She nods uncertainly. "I suppose it'll have to do."

All of a sudden, I want to hug her. She appears desolate; her entire orderly world turned upside down. I have no doubt she's an expert at what she does—she has to be, given her position in life—but no one, no matter how well-prepared or expert, is prepared for this.

"It'll be okay," I say because embracing her is out of the question. "I promise."

"Don't." She gives me one of her dagger-edged looks. "Don't promise. You can't. You have no idea what will happen, so don't pretend that you do. Let's just get on with it."

I don't have anything to reply to this. Luke Waverley, however, does. As she shoulders her bag, he leans to me to murmur, "She might look like a snowdrop, but she's made of uncuttable stone. Her father's daughter, Mr. Curtis. Don't ever forget it."

Chapter Six

Ania

We leave the Ritz like thieves ourselves, stealing out the Rue Cambon exit. Once we hail a cab near the Chanel boutique, Jerome turns to me with a mischievous smile; it's the first time a smile actually looks right on his face, making me think this is how he must have looked as a boy, whenever he did something he wasn't supposed to do.

"What now?" I ask, still wondering how he can think this is a good idea, never mind a safe one. We're on our own, with over half a million dollars of jewelry created by my father wrapped in underwear in my overnight bag.

"I have no idea. I don't know Paris well."

"And you think I do? I have an apartment here. It's where I stay. I'm only familiar with the hotels you'd expect me to know."

"Why not ask the cab driver?" he suggests, and when I stare at him through my sunglasses as if he's lost his mind—I'm starting to think he might have, and so have I to let him persuade me to this—he adds, "You'll have to ask. My French isn't great, either."

"Honestly." I say to the driver, "Can you recommend a hotel—?"

"A cheap one," Jerome interjects. "Tell him it has to be cheap."

"For heaven's sake, why?" I exclaim, causing the driver to smirk at us in the rearview mirror as if he's seen this a hundred times before: a foreign couple booted out of the Ritz for lack of sufficient funds, seeking economical alternatives. "I have plenty of money—"

"That's not the point." Jerome lights up a cigarette, to my disgust. "We don't want to look as if we have money, remember?"

I grit my teeth and relay to the driver, "A hotel on the Left Bank, please."

"I know just the place," the driver replies, again as if he's done this a hundred times before. "A friend of mine runs it. Breakfast included. Very nice. Clean."

"Not too nice or clean," Jerome says.

The driver gives Jerome a look in the mirror that makes me want to applaud.

"That sounds fine," I say. "Where, exactly?"

"In the Latin Quarter."

"Oh." I turn to Jerome. "Near the Sorbonne. Colorful. Lots of students."

"As long as we can disappear," he replies, blowing smoke out of the half-open taxi window. "And not so colorful as to draw attention to the princess-in-hiding."

"Now, listen up," I say, "I'm not a princess. And I'm warning you now, I'm not catching fleas on top of everything else. I can live without luxury. But there's absolutely no reason to live without a decent bathroom or a milled piece of soap. Or breakfast."

"As long as it's included in the price," he says, again with that boyish smile. He understands more French than he lets on. Probably speaks it better, too. The man is impossible. But I feel a rush of smug satisfaction. I've been taking orders from him all day. It's high time I put my foot down, even if that foot is now shod in ballet flats because I had to leave my heels on Luke's hotel bed.

We arrive at the Hotel de College du France. It's now close to ten p.m. There's still activity on the street in this part of the 5th arrondissement, filled with students, writers, artists, and red-painted cafés and restaurants that have been here forever. It's an ancient and famous section of the city, with an old square, and twisting cobblestone streets. A neighborhood where it feels as if time stopped and age-old traditions seep into the stone.

"It's called the Latin Quarter because of the language," I tell Jerome as he's not said another word, smoking and looking out the window as if he's pouting, except I know he's not. Pouting would indicate injured feelings, and I don't think he has any feelings that could be injured. "Latin was widely spoken at the University in the Middle Ages, after the twelfth-century philosopher Abelard took up residence here."

"Really?" He gives me a blank look.

"Pierre Abelard, the French philosopher?" I regard him, aghast. "Abelard and Heloise? You don't know the story?"

"Sorry. Must have missed it in one of my failed history classes."

"Oh my God." I roll my eyes. "Abelard was a theologian, renowned throughout Europe. He fell in love with Heloise—her uncle was a canon of Notre Dame, and she lived with him in a house near this quarter. She was also known for her knowledge of classical letters. Fluent in Latin, Hebrew, and Greek. They fell in love, but her uncle tried to separate them, so they had to secretly meet. When Heloise became pregnant, Abelard married her. After she gave birth to their son, it was a scandal, and her uncle threatened to ruin them, so Abelard sent Heloise into a convent—am I boring you?"

"Not at all." He's looking at me in such a way I can't tell if he's amused or mocking.

"Abelard wanted to protect her from her uncle, so Heloise dressed as a nun, though she didn't take any vows. Her uncle thought Abelard had forced her to enter the convent to be rid of her, so he had men break into Abelard's room and castrate him. Abelard later took vows as a monk at the monastery of St. Denis, but before he did, he insisted Heloise also take her vows as a nun. She sent him letters, asking him why she had to submit to a religious life she didn't want. Eventually, she took the vows and became an abbess. She's known today for being one of history's first women to protest patriarchy."

His eyes widen. "Pretty sad story, huh? Poor guy lost his balls."

"That's all you got from the story?" I say, smiling despite myself.

"Well." He narrows his gaze in a manner that I suddenly and very unexpectedly find too seductive for my own good. "You know what they say about boys and our balls."

"I do." I take out the fare from my wallet to pay the taxi driver. He gives us directions down the Rue d'Ecole to number 7 Rue Thénard, a non-descript, white, six-story building. Inside a wood-paneled reception area that's seen better days, the first thing I notice is a life-sized polychrome statue of St. Joan of Arc in the corner. A bit of kitsch and religion that for some reason, makes me feel better. It's a far cry from the Ritz or the Montalembert or the Lutecia, but as promised, decent enough.

And, hopefully, with two rooms available since I suddenly realize I'm exhausted.

The manager greets us in a typically understated French way. He only has one room available, he says, handing us the oversized brass key with its plastic tag.

Jerome shrugs and says, "I'll sleep on the floor." We climb the winding staircase to the cramped second floor.

It's certainly not the Ritz. Not even close. Two narrow beds that resemble cots, divided by a rickety table with an askew lamp. Drab wallpaper. A wardrobe with a door that won't shut all the way. A tiny, but to my immense relief, otherwise immaculate bathroom, though only a shower stall. No tub.

Jerome falls onto one of the beds. I eye him. I'm tempted to tell him I want to pull the beds together so he can just make himself comfortable with a pile of blankets on the floor as he suggested, but I know it'll sound petty.

"No smoking in here," I say instead, opening my bag on the other bed to remove my toiletries.

He starts up. "There's a window. And an ashtray."

"It's too small. You'll stink up everything. My clothes. My father's jewels. No."

He watches me go into the bathroom. The door is warped here, too. I can't close it.

"Too small?" I hear him say as I splash tepid water onto my face and regard my tired countenance in the mirror. I look like death. I'm carrying all the tension and anxiety under my eyes. "This room is about the size of my London flat."

"Well, then you can smoke in your London flat," I retort. "Not in here."

"Okay. I won't smoke." He rummages in his satchel, though I can't imagine what he possibly keeps in there, except for more cigarettes and maybe a pencil or two. After I wash off my makeup and apply much-needed moisturizer, I start to pull the pins from my chignon and stop. I can do that later. Before bed.

When I step back into the room, to my surprise, I find he's changed into a pair of jeans and a dark, slightly ragged turtleneck sweater, his suit discarded in a heap.

"Much better." He lets out a sigh. "I'm not made to be a fashion plate."

"Evidently." I think about changing into some fresh clothes myself—I've been in my Dior suit all day—but the very thought of having to remove the jewels to get to my clothing makes me feel ill. I can do it later, though later is right around the corner, given the time.

"So?" I say. "Now, what?"

"We spend the night," he replies as if it's a given.

"I know that. I mean, what's the plan *after* we spend the night?"

He frowns. "You really like everything catalogued and in its proper place, don't you?"

"Mr. Curtis—" I start to say.

He holds up his hand. "I thought we agreed. Jerome."

"Jerome." I force out a smile that feels taut on my lips. "Yes, I like to know what I'm doing. Especially when I have no idea. It is your plan, after all. Not mine."

"Ouch." He winces. "You don't pull any punches, either."

I regard him in silence. My mind is going in a million different directions, and I can't focus anymore. As tired as I am, I can't imagine I'll be able to get any sleep. I need to take a sleeping pill. But if I do, I'm afraid I won't be alert enough for whatever happens tomorrow.

"You'll call your driver first thing in the morning to tell him to pick up Mr. Cologne at the Ritz to take him to the bank," he says. "Then we call Mr. Cologne."

"He has a name. It's Luke. Luke Westerly. Stop calling him that."

"Yeah, well. Mr. Westerly doesn't like me very much."

"Don't be ridiculous. He likes you more than you think."

"Oh?" The tone in his voice suddenly causes me to laugh. My laughter sounds so strange: brittle in this room, as if I don't laugh often enough. "I hope not much more," he adds. "I don't swing that way."

"Again, don't be ridiculous. You're not his type."

"And you know this because…?"

"I've worked with him since I was nineteen. Believe me, I know. He prefers young gentlemen of distinction."

"Ah." Jerome waves his hand over his appearance. "Not schlubs like me."

"Precisely." I sit on the edge of the bed. To my dismay, in the resultant silence, I hear my stomach growl. He hears it, too.

"Food," he says. "We need food. A hearty dinner."

I almost scoff. "I'm fine. I ate on the plane—"

"You didn't eat. You pecked at a salad that wouldn't fill a mouse. I mean actual food, not those crustless cucumber sandwiches or a famous mini-club at the Carlton."

"You didn't eat the famous mini-club at the Carlton," I remind him.

"No. And I'm starving." He pats his lean stomach under his shapeless sweater.

"I'm not going anywhere." I meet his eyes, my hand reaching instinctively to my bag.

"Right." He nods. "I'll do it." He turns to the door. "Don't go anywhere."

I sigh. "I just said I wouldn't."

He leaves. All of a sudden, I'm alone for the first time since early this morning. For a few minutes, I can only sit there. Then I force myself to unzip my bag, carefully extract the clothes I need without disturbing the muffled jewels, and change into a pair of black drawstring trousers and a white cashmere pullover. I pace to the window, staring out over the crowded streets of the quarter, the spire of Notre Dame still visible in the distance, its silhouette limned by the city at night.

Paris. I've been here so many times, it's become a home, as familiar as New York or Los Angeles. The City of Lights. Of beauty and inspiration. The place I've often retreated to when I'm about to design a new collection. I remember coming to stay at our residence the spring after my mother died, devastated by her loss. The apartment has a balcony, only large enough for two people. Ivy spills over the side of the building and grows over the balustrade in tendrils; the balcony edged with planters that my mother filled with bulbs. That spring, the tulips were starting to bud in the planters, her final gift to me. I was so inspired by their nascent beauty and the message they imparted about the ephemerality of life that I designed a series of necklaces and bracelets using them as a motif. Pink sapphire and amethyst petals with long stems paved with tsavorites that wound around the neck or arm. The collection was a huge success. We sold every piece, and flowers became integral to my subsequent designs.

I look over my shoulder at my bag. See the jewels made by my father as if the leather exterior has turned transparent, each tucked in like children as Luke said, wrapped in my expensive lingerie and Hermès scarves. I must be crazy. What am I doing, hiding out in a cheap hotel room with the very jewels that should, at this moment, be adorning the clients I need to appease in order to save my business? *How* can this be happening to me?

I hear a knock on the door. Without thinking, I go to open it.

"No." Jerome steps inside, carrying a large paper bag. "You can't just open the door without knowing who it is first."

"I knew it was you," I say.

"But what if it wasn't?"

"Who else would it be? You left the key. Look. On the side table."

He glances at the table. "Huh. Not very smart of me, either."

I can't believe it, but I feel tears rise to choke me. I turn away from him and return to the window. Somewhere, not far away, I hear the music of an Edith Piaf record playing, her throaty melancholic lament wafting over the quarter. Well, isn't that just perfect?

I hear Jerome rustle in the bag, his exhale of effort, and then he comes up behind me. He hands me a water glass filled with red wine. "Probably not your preferred vintage."

I take a long sip and sigh. "Thank you."

"Come over here." I turn to see he's pulled down the coverlet of his bed and spread out a spare blanket, on top of which he's flattened the paper bag and set out two mounds wrapped in newsprint. "There's a vendor on the corner. Lamb falafels probably aren't your style, but I'm learning not to underestimate you."

And with those words, after everything that's happened, after an entire day of shock and anger, loss and panic and fear, he undoes me. I feel a tear slip down my cheek.

Jerome takes the glass from my hand. "It's okay," he whispers.

"No." I can barely speak. "It's not. Nothing is okay. None of it."

"It will be. I…" He falters.

"You, what?" I rub the back of my hand against my eyes, and for some absurd reason, I'm glad that I took off my mascara.

"I was going to say, 'I promise.'" He lowers his eyes. "But I can't."

"I appreciate it."

He lifts his face, a lock of his unruly hair tumbling over his forehead. He's a young man. No more than thirty-five or six. I can see it in the ease of his movements, the way he holds his thin yet strong frame. But there's old pain in his eyes, as if he's seen too much—too much to forget.

"I'd rather you didn't lie to me," I say. "Don't make promises. I never trust promises."

"No expectations and no promises," he repeats. "Aren't we a pair?"

"Let's eat." I pull myself together, and we sit on the bed, where he unwraps the mounds to reveal hunks of pita bread stuffed with what appears to be soggy French fries and inedible chunks of meat. It looks awful, but I make myself take a bite. Quite to my surprise, it's delicious. Greasy and too fattening, but delicious all the same.

"Guess I was right," he says as he devours his falafel.

"About?"

"Not underestimating you. The princess has a common appetite." He chuckles, and I like it now. Candid, as if he's as taken aback as much as I am to be enjoying himself.

"I like peanut butter and jelly, too," I say, finishing my falafel and pouring myself another generous serving of wine. "I'm not the delicate princess you think I am."

"You certainly aren't." He shakes his head. "Director of a world-famous jewelry company with a private plane. Attitude for days. Quite the appetite, too, from what I just saw. And so beautiful, it hurts to breathe." He goes still as his unexpected declaration thickens the air between us. "Sorry. That was uncalled for."

"What? That you just told me I have attitude for days?"

He starts digging into his pocket and pauses.

"Oh, go ahead," I say.

He lights a cigarette then goes to the window to blow out the smoke. At some point, he's taken off his shoes. He's not wearing any socks. He has long, bony feet. I'm riveted by the sight. When was the last time I saw a man's feet? I can't recall.

"That's a nasty habit," I say, picking up the detritus of our meal just to do something, storing the waste in the paper bag.

"You never smoke?" he asks.

"Never. My mother used to smoke. I think she died from it."

"I'm sorry." He flicks ash over the windowsill and instead scatters it on the floor. "We all gotta die from something, though."

"We do. But not like her." I crunch the top of the paper bag into a knot and drop it into the wire trash bin by the door.

He goes quiet as if he realizes he's been insensitive. "I started smoking in high school," he says in the sudden hush. "But I really started smoking during the war. It was what we did to pass the time, waiting for the Luftwaffe to dump bombs on us." He pauses again. "I'm really putting my foot in it, aren't I? Must be the wine. I don't drink very often."

"Neither do I." I regard him from the bed, my glass in hand. "Tell me about the war."

He crushes out his cigarette in the tin ashtray. "Forget I mentioned it."

I watch him pace to the other bed and contemplate my bag, his hands shoved into his jeans' pockets, the smell of his tobacco bitter in my nose. Not acrid. Pleasant, in a way. It reminds me of my childhood, of my mother's after-dinner cigarette.

"It must have been hard on you," I say. "If you can't even talk about it."

He glances up at me. In the lamp's muted light, shadow delineates the sharp bones of his face, the stubble on his cheeks painted black.

"It was." His voice is low. Then he strides over to me, takes the glass from my hand, puts it on the side table, and says, "I should go take a walk. Let you rest."

"Why?" I lift my eyes to his.

"Because." He swallows. "Because I very badly want to kiss you right now."

It's exactly what I don't need to hear. I know better than to succumb to a random temptation incited by too much wine and a need to escape. I know better than to allow any man— especially a stranger—to get the better of me. But I want him to, and that's the strangest, most unexpected thing of all. I don't care anymore if it's right or wrong. I don't care if I'll regret it. I see the same longing to be understood in him, the same fear that he might not be that I carry inside. And, somehow, I think he knows it. He sees it in me, too, in a way I never thought anyone would.

I stand up to face him, though I have to crane my head. "Do it, then."

"I can't." He looks as if he'll step back, but he doesn't. Outside the open window, another Piaf song floats into the violet air.

I give him a smile. "Why not? I can't think of a greater cliché. A May night in Paris. A robbery. A girl in trouble. A man who has to protect her. Cheap wine. An anonymous hotel. And Edith Piaf with tears in her voice. It's perfect. Like a movie." I start to laugh at the absurd irony of it.

And that's when he leans forward and kisses me.

His mouth tastes of wine and smoke, but his lips are supple. Hesitant at first, it takes me a moment before I press back suddenly, hungrier for him than I was for the food. Once again, I smell the faded pine embedded in his sweater. I think that if I lick his skin, I'll taste a forest. When his arms come around me, it's like a vise. For a second, I want to break free. But then I feel his ropy length, his deceptive slenderness as I lean farther into him.

I want to lose myself in his body. I want to feel all of him against me. I press into him until he falls onto the bed. Conversations from cafés in the streets below drift through the window, and Piaf sings. And then I feel the sudden chill on my shoulders as he removes my pullover, his urgency as he trails his lips down my neck to my collarbone, his unshaven skin rough against mine. Coarse in the way it should be, how I want it to be. But he's still being gentle as he reaches my breasts, deftly unhooking my brassiere without my noticing it, and then I think I'm going to explode with how slowly he moves, when all I want is a punishing embrace to quench the sting of everything gone wrong. Part of me wants this to go wrong, too. For this to be another mistake, but one I at least make willingly—until he pulls back, stares into my eyes, and says huskily, "Are you sure?"

"Yes," I reply.

He tears off his sweater as I reach for his jeans, peeling the worn denim from his narrow hips. He senses everything I want without my having to say a word. When I lower myself upon him, he thrusts into me. I suddenly think about the fact that we're not using any protection, but then I'm moaning at the intensity of it, the heat building inside me, and he's right there, coaxing me, watching me. Feeling me.

Skin upon skin. The sensation of touching every part that can be touched. He lets me take the lead, and I enjoy it, but something's missing. I don't want to tell him. This is my test. I need him to know what to do. It's always like this with the men I'm with. Something I must either say or do to guide him. I don't want that. I do it all day. I'm in charge of more than two dozen employees in a company. The very last thing I want in bed is to—

And then he does it. He pins my arms by my sides, looks at me, and whispers, "Stop it, Ania. Stop planning your next move. Stop thinking. Just feel it."

He climaxes while still holding my arms down. He shifts lower, bringing his mouth to me, his tongue darting, teasing. The pleasure is so exquisite, it's almost like pain. I try to extricate my arms from his grip. I want to touch him. I want to ravel my hands in his hair. But he holds me captive.

Stop thinking. Just feel it.

And then he slips back inside me and puts his lips, wet with my taste, on mine, and he kisses me as I explode. With Piaf still singing. Without a breath of air on our heated skin.

And I cry out because he knew what I needed. To be overcome. Overwhelmed. To not be in control for once in my life.

To not be in control at all.

Chapter Seven

Jerome

She falls asleep in my arms like an exhausted child, her tangled hair that smells of luxury flung across my chest, her taut body coiled against my ribs, sheathed in its warm white-silk skin. She doesn't look as thin naked, not that she couldn't use a few more falafels.

I should get some sleep, too. God knows I need it. But I can't believe I'm lying here with this woman, with the salt of her musk, her perfume and ardor, clinging to my hands.

Jerome Curtis, you rogue. You've just made love to a goddess.

I thought she'd kick me out when I told her I wanted to kiss her, let alone let me do any of this, but instead, her reaction was…well, I can't help but think it wasn't how a good girl is supposed to react. But then, what do I know? I don't have a ton of experience, with good girls or otherwise.

Romance was never part of my plan. I've seen enough marriages go awry to conclude it's the most unreasonable obligation we can impose on each other. My parents, for one, fought all the time until they divorced, and I had to live with my embittered mother, who moved back with me into her parent's home in Minnesota. My grandparents didn't have what you'd call an ideal marriage, either. My grandpa was injured and made to forcibly retire from his factory job, so he drank too much, while Grandma sacrificed so much of herself to raise their family, there was nothing left but a litany of, "More coffee, dear?" and endless baking for a continuous rotation of auxiliary garden clubs.

As soon as I could go to college, I found one clear across the country. I majored in business administration, one of those nonsensical degrees for any rut of a job. Then I applied for a position in the Federal Bureau of Investigation in Washington D.C., mostly filing papers at first until I proved I could do more and was assigned to assist in minor investigative work. I was twenty-two years old when Japan attacked Pearl Harbor. By then, Hitler had Europe under assault, and I was dating a secretary in the Bureau who believed we were engaged. Imagine her surprise when I told her I was enlisting to fight, like thousands of other American boys. Trying to explain that I had to go, so either I enlisted now or got drafted was like trying to convince a wailing wall. She refused to countenance that her pink dream of picket fences, two perfect children, and a golden retriever was going up in smoke with the rest of the world.

I couldn't board my first aircraft carrier fast enough. I thought I'd be sent to serve in the Pacific. However, due to my experience in the F.B.I, they dispatched me to Europe as part of a reconnaissance unit, charged with severing enemy lines of communication and investigating a series of blurry aerial photographs taken by the Free French, who insisted the complexes were forced-labor camps. Seven years of war and its gruesome aftermath. I never returned to the United States. After my unit was discharged, I found work as an insurance investigator in London, where I at least spoke the language.

The rest, as they say, is history.

Ania shifts. I tighten my hold on her, craving a cigarette at the same time. As I slowly reach for the packet on the side table, her syrupy sleep voice says, "You have a scar."

I go still, then make myself extract a cigarette from the pack. She uncoils from my side, pushing tangled hair from her face. Such a face. Without any makeup, her lips slightly bruised from my stubble, and her eyes drowsy, she looks half her age.

"Here." Her fingertip sends an electric jolt through me as she traces the ridge of scar tissue on my stomach. "Is this from one of those Luftwaffe bombs?"

I inhale and expel the smoke through the side of my mouth, away from her. It hovers in the darkness above us like a dissipating cloud. Or a ghost.

"No," I finally say.

She lets out a sigh I can't decipher, then starts pulling back the rumpled bed covers when I put my hand on her gorgeous back, her rib cage palpable under her skin.

"Don't."

"I'll be right back." She pads into the bathroom. I move upright in the bed, tapping ash into my palm until she returns, gives me a look, and retrieves the tin ashtray by the windowsill. Then she takes up my turtleneck sweater and pulls it on, its tube collar sliding over her head, its worn heft billowing on her. I feel myself start to harden. That mass of blond hair, like a mane framing her cat-agate eyes, those incredible ballerina legs…

Jerome, my old chap. You're in serious trouble.

"It's from afterwards," I hear myself say. "The scar. I was stabbed."

She perches on the bedside. Doesn't say anything, but I see the question in her eyes. I can't avoid it. And to my discomfort, I realize I don't want to.

"Darcy and I…" I cough and stub out the cigarette. I feel my arms wrap about my midriff as if I'm trying to hide the scar. I'm not, but I am attempting to hide something. "We served together. After it ended, we volunteered for a secret unit."

"Why was it secret?"

"Because it was an intelligence operation. Germany was in ruins. Everything flattened by the Allied bombings. So was most of Europe. Refugees everywhere, clamoring to get into France, cross the Channel to Britain, emigrating to America. It was…"

"Chaotic, I imagine," she says. "I was sixteen when the war ended, but I remember reading about it in the newspapers. All those poor people. It broke my heart."

"Yeah." I light another cigarette. "It didn't break as many hearts as it should have. Quotas were set. Visas became a lottery of who-can-bribe-whom. No one wanted destitute survivors or emaciated Jews arriving on their doorstep." As I see her wince at my words, I say, "Anyway. Among all those poor people cramming bombed-out roadways or scavenging for food in bombed-out cities, were others equally as desperate, who needed to be caught."

"Nazis," she says quietly.

"Yes. We had lists. Like them. You wouldn't believe how many did it willingly. How many actually agreed with it." I hear the anger in my voice that's never fully deserted me, even as I try to curb it. "They were trying to escape, too. To South America. Asia. Anywhere they could hide and become someone else. Some of them, the higher-ups, we knew would be impossible to catch unless we moved fast. But others…"

She moves. I think she's going to take my hand. I can't bear it. I clamp my hands under my arms about my torso, but she doesn't reach for them. She plucks the cigarette dangling from my mouth and extinguishes it in the ashtray.

"We apprehended about twenty of them," I go on. "Sometimes, they fought back. A woman who'd been a guard at Ravensbruck stabbed me with a broken bottle while trying to get away. A superficial wound, but it left a scar. Then came Dessau."

"Dessau. Is that where it happened? With Darcy?"

I nod. "Our target was a low-level shit. A former notary. A paper-pusher. He was responsible for deporting over five thousand to the camps in Poland. Darcy killed him. I let him do it and then helped him cover it up."

In the ensuing silence, she doesn't move. Doesn't blink. Her eyes remain focused on me, and I think…this is it. Now she knows she's in serious trouble, too.

"I would have done the same," she eventually says.

Now, *I'm* the one who cannot move.

"We would have been court-marshaled," I say as if I must test her, thrust the burden of it on her and see if what she claims is actually true. "Our mission was to investigate their whereabouts, hunt them down, and arrest them for sentencing at Nuremberg or another international court. Not murder them."

"But they murdered other people. An eye for an eye."

I almost laugh, except it's not funny. "You really do have diamond dust in your veins."

She turns her head to look toward the window. "So. That's how Darcy was blackmailed. The Leopard found out." When I don't speak, she glances at me. "He knows about you, too. Doesn't he? About how you covered it up."

"Yes." I swallow. "I guess you could say I'm a liability."

Her smile is barely a smile at all. "Not to me."

"Ania." I uncross my arms, reach out to set my hand on her leg. "Two men in your employ murdered a Nazi while under covert service for the U.S. government. Trust me, I *am* a liability."

"You're not in my employ," she replies.

"Right." I start to lean back. "Neither is Darcy. My mistake."

"No." She clasps my hand before I can remove it. "Darcy is still my employee. Now, more than ever. As for you…" She inclines to put her lips on my mouth, her other hand searching under the covers. "You work for Lambert Securities. It's their problem. As long as you do your job, what you did before is not my concern."

I gasp as she finds me, but my fingers close around her wrist. "And this?" I ask her.

"This?" Her eyes dim. I see the remoteness resurface in their depths.

"This," I say, my voice gone hoarse. "Us. You know what I mean."

"It is what it is. Don't promise. Don't expect. I can't deal with anything else."

I release her wrist, then let her bring down the covers and do what she wants.

You don't refuse a goddess.

I wake to sunlight streaming through the window, feeling more refreshed than I have in years. And sore. As I rise and go to pee, it burns a bit. I look at my member and chuckle. *You need to get out more often, my friend.*

She's not in the room, which plunges me into panic. But her bag is still by the bed where we toppled it in our rush to get at each other. After a quick shower and shave, just as I'm pulling on my turtleneck and jeans, wondering where in the hell she is and where the hell my comb disappeared to, she returns with a tray, laden with two big white mugs and a plate of croissants. Like a waitress. If waitresses wore slim blue slacks molded to their thighs, crisp white blouses, and expressions of utter disregard for my disbelief.

"*Where* did you go?"

She puts the tray on the bed. "To get our breakfast. It's included in the price."

"Christ." I grab my wristwatch from the side table. "It's already—oh. Only seven-twenty-five."

"I didn't want to wake you." She hands me one of the mugs. "You looked so peaceful asleep. Not like you at all."

The hot coffee scalds my mouth. "What time do banks open here?"

"Nine o'clock." She uses a blunt butter knife on the tray to slice open the croissants and spread jam into their flaky insides. I wonder when she last had to fetch her own breakfast or serve it. I would bet it's been a very long time—if ever. "I also used the reception phone. Henri can pick up Luke at any time. I didn't call Luke," she adds, as I eye her over the croissant. "I didn't know what to say. Your plan, remember?"

I bite into the croissant. "We have to find a car. A rental. Can we do that?"

"I believe so." She eats delicately, her croissant folded into a napkin. The rich girl who doesn't want to stain her blouse. "You can rent cars in Paris. Not that I've ever found the need."

"We rent a car and drive to the Ritz, but not up to the hotel," I continue, ignoring her dry statement. "Then we call Luke. He's to take the cases to the bank with Henri, and we have to know exactly when they leave so we can follow them. That exit we took from the hotel yesterday is a good place for Henri to pick Luke up. But…"

"But?" She sips her coffee. Almost unperturbed, as if I'm describing a day of sightseeing.

"We need a phone to call from. We can set a time in advance for Luke to leave the hotel, but there might be traffic on our way there. Paris has a lot of traffic, right?"

"Like any major city. We can call him from the Chanel boutique. All the salesgirls know me. I keep a standing account there."

Of course, she does.

"Okay. I guess that'll work." I gulp my coffee, welcoming the warm burst in my belly.

"Another croissant?" She motions to the tray.

"Cut it out," I grumble.

She laughs. "There's the Mr. Curtis I know." And the way she says it, so matter-of-factly, makes me want to smear jam all over her naked body and lick it off. But she's already turning to her bag, folding up her clothes from last night.

"Almost eight o'clock," she says. "I suggest you take a shower. And that suit of yours on the floor isn't going to pack itself."

Chapter Eight

Ania

Jerome waits outside in the rental while I walk up to the boutique on Rue Cambon and ring the bell. It's not opening for another two hours, but I know Madame Berger, the boutique manager. She always arrives promptly at eight a.m. sharp because I once had to pick up a little black suit for an early meeting.

Seeing me through the glass window, she unlocks the door to usher me inside. The soothing black-and-beige interior and associates setting up the day, all dressed in outfits designed by Chanel, make me feel, for the moment at least, as if the world has returned to its proper order. The fate of so much I've worked for and care about hinges on Jerome's plan. But here in this rarefied shop scented with signature No. 5, everything feels right again. Here, nothing feels as if it could ever go wrong.

I smile as the salesgirls greet me. I wish I could have slipped in incognito, but if I weren't a well-known, longtime customer, I wouldn't be granted the privilege of having the store opened for me before hours or the use of the manager's office to make a private call.

When I explain to Madame Berger, she motions me into her domain. A small, exquisite office echoing the boutique's black-and-beige motif, its sole concession to color a vivid purple orchid on her desk—in a black lacquer pot with the iconic, entwined CC logo. Madame leaves me alone.

I've barely picked up the handset to dial the Ritz switchboard when her secretary enters quietly to place a tiny cup of espresso—in keeping with the boutique's theme, the cup a cream china with black trim—in front of me and tiptoes out again. As I wait for my call to connect, I sip the aromatic brew. I'll have to be sure to buy something the next time I'm here. I could use a new red bag to go with my red Vivier pumps, currently in Luke's hotel room.

One of the unexpected oddities of my predicament is that I find I really miss my shoes. I'm taller than the average woman, so flats should be my style, but I've always preferred heels. I like the advantage it gives me over the men in my business that I must contend with, those who start off thinking I'm too pretty or fragile to drive a hard bargain at the table. First, they're taken aback that I stare them directly in the eyes. Then I throw them further off balance by the acumen of my knowledge, so they start to think twice about overcharging me for stones or a new account or advertisement placement. Before they even know it, I'm no longer just Virgil Thorne's daughter, his hastily appointed replacement. I'm the person they must satisfy in order to make their money. High heels may be shoes to most women, but they're weapons to me.

Even as I contemplate it, I marvel at my ability to even think about shoes at a time like this. Which leads to my escapade of last night. It sears my memory. For a moment, I close my eyes to marvel at that, too.

I lost control. On purpose. I wanted to throw caution to the wind, but I didn't anticipate what came next. In the past, whenever I was with a man, I always knew the ultimate result. It was never meant to go beyond a few dates, a few nights. Again, it's not how a woman might be expected to behave, but in this respect, I am very much Virgil Thorne's daughter. I've never met a man who could compare to my father, nor any whom I felt worthy of the effort. I never believed any man could be my match and came to terms with that fact. I understood the sacrifices I would have to make by assuming my father's role in the company. Men might fantasize about an independent woman in the bedroom, but they rarely want one in real life—and certainly not outside the bedroom. It's threatening to them. And when men feel threatened, it creates fear. And fear inevitably leads to resentment.

But Jerome…he isn't threatened by me. He's not afraid. If anything, I think I might be more scared of *him*. Of what he could do to my painstaking vision of how my life should be.

"Hello?" Luke answers the call.

"It's me," I say.

"Darling. Did you have a good night in whatever vermin-infested hole that entirely unsuitable but devastatingly attractive new friend of yours insisted you stay in?"

I have to smile. "It was actually a nice hotel. In the Latin Quarter. Not bad at all."

"But not the Ritz."

"No," I concede. "I survived it."

"Naturally. That's what you are: a survivor. Now, tell me, what role am I slated to play in this cloak-and-dagger affair? I'm dying of curiosity."

I proceed to give him the instructions. After a moment of silence, he says, sounding somewhat disappointed, "That's all? Take the cases to the bank vault in your car?"

"Luke, it might be dangerous. Jerome believes the thief could try to steal those cases en route. He bribed or hired someone at Orly to inspect the plane, to ascertain how many cases were brought, and we failed to go to my residence last night. My car on its way to the bank is the thief's likely target. Taking the cases there—"

"Is like waving a red flag before the bull. And I love matadors." Luke's sudden laugh eases the knot in my chest. He's always been unflappable. I've never once seen him lose his equanimity. Of all the men I've known, he's the one I most admire after my father.

"And you and he will be…?" Luke asks.

"Yes," I reply.

"And you're quite sure you know what you're doing? Your Mr. Curtis might be very good with that gun of his, my sweet, but it is just one gun."

"Jerome is sure."

"Oh, he is?" Luke laughs again. "Well, then. Say nothing more. The surly Mr. Curtis will surely protect us from an unexpected rampage. So, when precisely should I leave this glorious establishment for the perilous wilds of Paris?"

"I need to call Henri. I've mapped out a route for him, so if we lose sight of you, we can still stay as close as possible. Call me back at the Chanel boutique in, say, five minutes?"

"You're at Chanel? Why, you're just down the street. Very well, I'll ring you there."

He hangs up, and I take another sip of espresso, feeling the caffeine jolt in my veins. I dial Henri's number and get his estimated time of arrival at the Ritz. Time seems to slow to a crawl before the phone rings. I don't answer it, as the call could be for the store.

Madame Berger's secretary looks in. "For you, Mademoiselle Thorne."

I pick up the receiver. "In fifteen minutes," I tell Luke. "Rue Cambon exit."

After thanking Madame on my way out of the shop, I notice a lovely quilted red bag with an interlocking chain strap on the display. That one will do nicely.

"Everything set?" Jerome asks when I get into the rental Fiat. He's been smoking, and I lower the window to let the cloud of smoke out.

"Yes. Henri is picking Luke up in about fifteen minutes."

We sit quietly.

"I'm so nervous," I hear myself say.

He reaches out to squeeze my hand. When he feels me flinch, he asks, "Okay with this?"

"No," I say. "Are you?"

He smiles that boyish smile that crinkles his eyes. "I was just thinking how twenty-four hours ago, I would never, in a million years, have imagined any of this."

"I suppose every cloud has its silver lining."

"You think I'm a silver lining? I'm flattered. I always thought I was the pewter type."

"Honestly." I have to laugh.

We sit quietly again, both of us watching the street and the hotel exit. A car pulls up. I tense. But it's not my vehicle. It's another Renault 5, from which a svelte, elderly woman in a tweed Chanel suit gets out to walk into the Ritz. The R5 drives off.

"Aren't you nervous?" I ask him.

"My job doesn't allow me to be nervous."

"Never?"

"Well. Last night. That made me nervous."

"Last night wasn't a job for you, was it?" I say.

"It certainly wasn't, princess. But it still made me nervous."

"Please don't call me that." My voice is harsher than I mean it to be.

He gives me a look. "Is there a reason for this aversion to being called a princess?"

"Yes, but not one I'm in any frame of mind to share right now."

"Okay. I'll just find you another nickname."

"How about you stick with Ania?"

"Fine. Ania, relax."

"*Relax?* How about you—" My irate retort is interrupted by my car pulling up to the curb in front of the Ritz. Henri gets out. Luke emerges moments later, two of the cases in each hand, and slides into the back seat as Henri holds open the door for him. As they pull out and drive past us parked by the sidewalk, I see Jerome check his rearview mirror. He might not be nervous, but his hands grip the steering wheel so tightly, his knuckles turn white, and his entire posture has gone rigid as if he's about to spring—like when he saw the necklace tumble out of the envelope onto my salad in the Carlton.

"What is it?" I whisper.

He replies in a flat voice, "I'm looking to see if anyone is following them. Let's go."

My stomach lurches as he shifts gears and moves the car out into the street, trailing Henri. It should take about twenty minutes to reach the Société Generale Bank at 91 Avenue des Champs-Élysées in the 8th arrondissement, not far from Avenue Montaigne where my residence is located. We are on Rue Rivoli now, and thus far, traffic isn't bad. But as we turn left and continue into the treacherous Place de la Concorde, we enter the morning rush. Harried people making their way to work and the usual stampede of taxis zipping in and out of traffic. We almost lose sight of my car ahead, but Jerome's an excellent driver, even under pressure. Until a Citroen edges into our lane, and he has to slam on the brakes to avoid a collision. A barrage of cars blast horns at us. The stoplight ahead turns red.

Jerome curses. "Damnit. We're going to lose them."

As soon as the light turns green, he speeds up onto Cours la Reine, which runs alongside a park. Traffic is against us, but to my relief, I spot my car ahead.

"There," I say.

Jerome gives a grim nod. "I see them."

We're only a half-dozen or so cars behind when Henri makes the slight right turn onto Rue François 1er. Jerome starts to make the same turn when, out of nowhere, a motorcycle shoots out from behind us and roars past, an ebony streak to my right, expelling a noxious spew of exhaust.

"What the hell...?" I hear Jerome say, Seconds later, cacophony erupts. A screech of brakes, horns blaring. Traffic coming to an abrupt standstill in front of us.

Jerome looks at me. Just one look, and it freezes me where I sit. Not wasting a minute, he pulls the car to the curb, yanks open his door, and leaps out, shouting at me, "Get your bag! Follow me, but not too close. If you see anything suspicious, go into the nearest public place."

I grab my bag as he takes off running. He's so fast, faster than I can possibly hope to be in ballet flats, hauling an overnight bag crammed with jewels and clothes, but I try my best to keep sight of him, even as fear starts to smother my lungs. In the halted traffic, I see drivers leaning out their windows, staring and pointing ahead.

"*Un accident*," I hear as I run past them.

An accident.

I pull my bag up higher on my shoulder, feeling it dig into my sides, my chest burning as I stagger past startled pedestrians on the sidewalk, standing up from the little tables outside the cafés, and then I see my car across the intersection, wedged between splintered trees, its front end crushed into the retaining wall girdling the steep drop to the roadway below.

I can't breathe at all. As I pause to gulp air through my mouth, my throat so tight it feels as if an invisible noose is strangling me, I hear the sound of an engine. In a flash, what appears to be the same motorcycle that burst past us earlier backs out from between the shattered trees, bounces onto the road ahead, and zooms off.

I try to focus on it, thinking it's important to see the driver. Is it the same motorcycle that passed us a while back? I can't tell. Everything is happening too fast; all I can see is that the driver is dressed in black with a helmet. The motorbike is black. He could be anyone, any of the innumerable men in Paris who drive motorcycles.

Then I realize what's happened and rush to my smashed-up vehicle. Jerome is kneeling at the driver's side, his fingers on Henri's wrist, testing his pulse. Henri sits slumped in his seat, his eyes closed, his face colorless.

"Oh, God," I whisper. "No…"

Jerome motions urgently to me. "He's unconscious. From the impact. He might have a concussion. Check on Luke."

I turn to the rear door of the car, yanking at the handle. Inside, Luke is sprawled across the back seat, a deep gash on his forehead. I'm still holding my bag, gripping it like a life preserver, but I make myself drop it to lean into the car.

"Luke. Luke, please. Are you all right?"

He gives me a sickly smile. "Not quite, darling. But I can see you and hear you, so I imagine it's not fatal. I am a bit out of sorts. What about poor Henri?"

"Just sit still," I say. "Jerome is with Henri."

"We need an ambulance," Jerome says. "He needs to go to a hospital. They both do."

"A hospital?" Luke tries to right himself and moans, lifting a hand to his gashed forehead. "I assure you, I'm perfectly…" He falls back against the seat. As I anxiously reach for his hand, he whispers, "Perhaps your Mr. Curtis is right."

"I'll find a phone." I straighten, frantically look around. The cafés across the street. Someone will let me call. I'm about to dash across the intersection when I see a police car pull up. A gendarme jumps from the car and crosses the street to me.

"Is anyone hurt?" he asks.

"My driver and my business associate." I hear the sob in the back of my throat. Not now. I can't fall apart now.

"An ambulance is on its way, mademoiselle. Please step aside and allow me to see if there's anything I can do until it arrives."

I follow him, quickly retrieving my overnight bag by the car. As the policeman examines Henri, Jerome catches my eye and glances toward the near-toppled trees, the only barrier that prevented the car from hitting the retaining wall at full speed and plunging into the crowded motorway far below. The fall would have killed them.

Two of the cases are tossed on the ground. I pick them up, feeling their lightness.

Henri says something to the gendarme that I can't hear. Overwhelming relief floods me. He's awake. Conversing.

I hand my bag and the cases to Jerome, sliding into the backseat where Luke is pressing his handkerchief to his wound. It's soaked in blood. I pull my scarf from my neck and dab at Luke's forehead. He's bleeding too much. He needs stitches.

"Thank you," Luke says. "Your lovely scarf will be ruined. I'm a dreadful imposition."

"Luke, don't say that. This is all my fault." My voice breaks.

"No, no. None of that. Henri will be fine. I will be fine after this nasty bruise is seen to. Don't waste your tears on us. Not when you have something much worse to lament."

"What?" I meet his sardonic regard. Only Luke could look amused in the midst of catastrophe.

"He managed to get two of the cases. The ones I refused to part with."

"You could have been killed!" I exclaim. "Who cares about two empty cases?"

"I'm afraid they weren't empty. You see, I tore out the linings and filled them with your shoes so they'd feel heavier. And I know how much you care about your shoes."

The ambulance arrives. Henri and Luke are put on stretchers to be taken to the nearest hospital. I want to ride with them, but the medics inform me it's not possible, so once I extract my car papers from the crumpled glovebox and address the necessary questions for the gendarme, who annotates everything, I return with Jerome to our rental, tilted halfway up on the curb where we left it.

He doesn't speak until we've pulled back into the clog of traffic, now cleared for passage past the accident site, and I give him directions on how to reach the hospital.

Then he says, "We shouldn't have done it. I didn't think it through."

"You couldn't have known," I reply haltingly, though now that the shock is starting to wear off, I think we really shouldn't have, and clearly, he didn't.

He stares at the road ahead. "Don't make excuses for me. I knew what he was capable of. I suspected he'd try to get to those cases on the way to the bank. I just didn't think he'd actually—" His jaw clenches, and I see the bone protrude under his skin. "So brazen. In full daylight. On a motorcycle in the middle of Paris. He's never done anything like this."

"So, it was him on that motorbike?" I ask, though I know it must have been.

"Yes." Jerome turns left at my indication. "I reached the car just as he was leaving. I looked right at him, Ania. The visor on his helmet was down so I couldn't see his face, but I saw the cases at his feet. He must have already strapped the missing ones to his bike. In less than six minutes, he caused an accident and took two cases." He bangs his open palm on the steering wheel. "Six goddamn minutes! How is it even possible? He was right there, too—in front of me, and I didn't lunge at him. I let him get away."

"You had to help Luke and Henri." My voice quavers.

"I did." He doesn't sound as if it makes him feel any better.

"Luke told me he tried to keep him from taking the cases."

"That was very gallant and stupid of him," says Jerome.

"The reason he took those cases is because they felt heavier. Luke took out the linings and filled them with my shoes."

"What?" He gives me an incredulous glance. "Your *shoes?*" A burst of sudden laughter escapes him. "Boy is he in for a surprise when he opens them."

I stare at him. "None of this is funny."

He turns somber. "You're right. It's not."

We continue to drive in uncomfortable silence before I say, "What now?"

He doesn't answer for a long moment. When he does, his voice is subdued. "I don't know. He's way ahead of us. He has a plan. When he finds out what's in those cases, he's not going to like it. We need to get your jewels into the vault before he makes another move."

"You think the vault will be safe enough?" Because, right now, there isn't a place in the entire world that feels safe enough. Not anymore.

"He's never stolen from a bank. Banks are too well guarded, too many obstacles to overcome. He steals from jewelers and jewel cutters, from exhibits and private persons. Not banks."

"But you just said he's never done anything like this. And, in Cannes, you said he'd changed his pattern."

"He has. This isn't how he operates. But breaking into a bank vault? I don't think even he'll dare go that far. He's always been a one-person show, at least for his heists. We suspect that, afterwards, he has some kind of international ring to fence the loot via underground channels, to dismantle the stones and sell them. But we've never recovered anything he's taken so…it's just an assumption. For all we know, he has a hideout somewhere piled with jewelry worth millions of dollars, like some modern-day Scrooge."

I tighten my grip on my bag in my lap.

"No leads," Jerome goes on, pulling into the circle before the hospital emergency entrance. "No idea where or when he'll strike next. I messed up big-time, and in less than twenty-four hours, I have to file my report with Lambert. They're not going to be happy with me. The news about Cannes must be in every newspaper by now. It'll just make finding him more difficult. He likes the publicity because he knows it complicates everything. Adds to the misinformation, which helps him disappear even easier." He stops the car. "Go ahead while I find a parking space."

As I reach for the door handle, he says, "I'm sorry, Ania."

I look at him. I want to tell him it's not his fault, but I can't. From the initial shock, I've descended into implacable resolve. I was right to think this was a crazy idea.

"I'm going to check on Luke and Henri," I tell him. "Then we're going to the bank to deposit the jewels. After that, I'm returning to my residence, where I have fresh clothes, extra pairs of shoes, and my own bed. I'm calling New York to order increased security measures at our stores. And then I'm filing my insurance claim with you for Cannes."

"Ania." He starts to reach for me but doesn't actually touch me again. "We've not reached that point yet. Filing the claim will mean you've accepted the loss. It'll signal that we've given up, when there's still a chance we can recover your jewels."

"We?" I open the door. "This man has attacked and injured three of my employees. My job now is to protect my company, Mr. Curtis. Your job is to recover my jewels—if you can. Which I highly doubt."

I move into the hospital. I know he's watching me, and I've hurt him. It hurts me, too, much more than it should. Much more than I expected.

But I'm Virgil Thorne's daughter. In the end, that's all I know how to be.

Chapter Nine

Jerome

I watch her stride into the hospital, her bag clutched to her side, and realize that I now know what it means when people say their heart sinks to their feet.

My job now is to protect my company, Mr. Curtis.

Mr. Curtis again. Not Jerome.

I understand. She must look after her interests, safeguard what she has left. She can always design new jewelry. She'll eventually receive a payment from the insurance claim and salvage the company if she works hard enough. I admire her resilience, her refusal to let this setback defeat her, but I still feel as if I've been punched right in the gut. Only last night, I was holding her in my arms. It seems like a thousand years ago.

I circle the hospital in search of a parking space. Once I locate one, I turn off the engine and smoke a cigarette, trying to pull myself together.

I've never been this close to catching the Leopard after years of pursuit, of poring over the unsolved case reports: his elusive entry completely unseen at night to remove a suite of peerless matched sapphires from a supposedly impenetrable exhibit in Shanghai. His unlocking of doors into a jeweler's exclusive shop, bypassing an allegedly impassable alarm system, to remove a ransom in jewels not yet presented to the jeweler's clientele. His slicing through the bulletproof glass window of the Madrid palace of a ducal heiress, depriving her of an antique set of heirloom emeralds. The heist in London and murder of the jewel cutter's assistant. And others, not directly attributed, but which I suspect are also his work. He left his mark in every incident linked to him: a leopard-print glove, hidden in a far corner above a wall or tucked under a floorboard, as if to dare the police to find it. In the other cases, the glove was never reported, but that doesn't mean it wasn't there. It just wasn't found.

Until London. There was no glove in London. Because he killed a woman.

After that, nothing. Six years of absence, during which his potential targets heaved a collective sigh of relief, interpreting his disappearance as proof that he'd either gotten away with enough loot to retire in unimaginable wealth—he had—or was killed by whomever he employed to launder the stolen goods—unlikely, given his rate of success. But no one except me believed he'd decided to lie low and wait for the next opportunity, the one guaranteed to splash his name in headlines again across the globe: the heist in Cannes.

I don't think he's done with Ania Thorne. He went after her replacements in broad daylight, pieces of historical value to her company. He won't give up now. For a reason that both confounds and disturbs me, he's intent on delivering a message to Thorne & Company, the most lauded jeweler in the U.S., from which he's never stolen until now.

He wants the world to know that no jeweler is safe from him.

I lock the car and go into the hospital. Henri is still being attended to in emergency, but Luke has been transferred upstairs. When I enter the room, Ania glances at me, and I hear her say to him, "You have to stay overnight, Luke. For observation. That's a bad head wound. The doctor says complications could arise."

"Any complications that arise will involve my intolerance for hospital gowns and hospital food," Luke replies tartly.

I have to smile. The guy might look like an Upper East Side snob, but he's no slouch.

"Do it for me," Ania says. "I insist. Just for tonight."

Luke sighs, his forehead swathed in bandages, but otherwise his droll self. "Wherever are my clothes, I wonder? That suit cost a considerable sum, and my wristwatch is vintage Thorne. I hope the hospital hasn't incinerated them along with its taste in decor."

"Everything is right there." Ania gestures to a set of lockers against the wall. "I made sure to tell the staff to secure all your belongings for when you're discharged."

"Darling, once again, I am in your debt."

"Don't be silly." She leans over the bed to kiss his cheek. I'm taken aback. Was I wrong about him? But then I see by the way his hand lifts briefly to caress her face that there's nothing sexual in his gesture. Their exchange is familiar. Familial.

"Do have a care, Ania. Try to get some rest if you can," he says. "You look terrible. It's only shoes. Shoes can be replaced."

She laughs, but there's no humor in it. She's putting up a brave front for his sake, and he's right: she looks ashen, blood spotting her blouse from tending to him in the car.

"Go now," he urges. "See to Henri. That poor man. He really did exert a monumental effort to keep us on the road. But the brute veered right in front of us, so we really had no other option than to hit the trees or another car. I feel awful that he bore the brunt of it."

Ania hesitates before she turns away. As she walks past me, I search her face, try to catch her gaze. She avoids it. "Please stay with Luke until I return," she says.

"Yes, of course." Helplessness overcomes me as she departs.

Luke chuckles. "Mr. Curtis, don't look so forlorn. Between the two of you, I feel as if I'm about to attend my own funeral."

I return his regard. "I'm really sorry about all this."

"Why? You didn't force me to do it at gunpoint. I volunteered." Luke pauses. "Well, not *volunteered*, precisely, but I was certainly a willing recruit. I must say, I enjoyed the high drama, if not the unexpected finale. I don't blame you in the slightest."

"You should," I reply.

"I'd do anything for Ania." His expression turns serious. "She's like a daughter to me. Or rather, a beloved niece. I've known her since she was a child. Virgil would often bring her to work with him. She was the most curious, rebellious little thing you can imagine. I adored her. Everyone at the company did, though none as much as her father. You could plainly see that for him, the sun rose and set on his daughter."

I don't know what to say. For the first time, it suddenly hits me how foreign this ultra-privileged world of high-end jewelry making is to me, of loving fathers and adored daughters. How I don't fit in at all in Ania Thorne's expensive, pampered life.

"Come now." Luke breaks into my thoughts. "You made the best call for the situation at hand. Surely, you can't be faulted for failing to anticipate every possible outcome. And you did safeguard our replacements, not an inconsiderable victory under the circumstances. I rather think we should be celebrating. Do they serve champagne in French hospitals? I imagine not."

"Why did you fight over the cases? Ania told me you refused to part with them. You risked your life for her shoes?"

His keen blue eyes focus on me. "Why do you think?"

"To make him believe the jewels were actually inside the cases."

"Exactly. I wasn't about to give them up when I knew Ania was a traffic stall away, carrying everything in her bag. I also believed that if I kept him engaged, trying to pry the cases from me, perhaps you'd arrive in time with your sturdy pistol to save the day."

"No such luck," I mutter.

"Unfortunately. Would you mind fetching me something from that dreadfully utilitarian locker? In my trousers. The right pocket, I believe."

I move to the locker and search through the plastic bag stuffed with his clothes. When I find the item crumpled in his pants pocket, I can't move for a second. Then I lift my eyes to him. He smiles. "See? Not all is lost."

"How...?" I lower my stare at the blood-crusted black glove in my hand.

"He was trying to hit me over the head. I had to grasp his wrist to detain him from finishing me off. The glove came away in the struggle, and he was too eager in that moment to seize the cases I let go of to notice I had a piece of evidence. It is evidence, isn't it? It can be dusted for fingerprints or some other boring procedure?"

I shake my head. "Sorry. Your blood is all over it. And he never leaves fingerprints."

"Not even inside a glove? How odd. I assure you, I saw his hand. It was quite bare. Well, other than..."

Something in his voice, lurking under that careless tone as if he's discussing the selection of canapes at a cocktail party, gives me pause.

"Other than what? What aren't you saying?"

Luke Westerly glances at the ajar room door. "I don't want Ania to hear."

I step close to his bed. "What don't you want her to hear?"

He draws in a troubled breath. "He had a ring on his index finger. A rare type of silver ring. With an intaglio onyx stone. Are you familiar with the term?"

"Not really."

"Intaglio carvings are cut into the gemstone to create the illusion of relief. It's known as *cavo-rilievo*, or sunken relief. You can think of it as the opposite of a cameo, where the relief of the design is tactile, protruding slightly from the stone's surface."

"That's rare?"

"Not the process itself. It's been popular since ancient times. However, I recognized this particular intaglio because it's very rare, indeed. It's from ancient Rome. Of the Etruscan goddess Laverna, patroness of thieves and the underworld. In Rome, her sanctuary was near the Porta Lavernalis."

I feel myself frown. "Why is that rare?"

"An onyx ring from the Romanic era? Mr. Curtis, such pieces are considered antiquities and of extreme value. The majority are in museums, with only a handful still among private collectors." He pauses as though it's an effort to divulge what he says next. "In all my years in this business, I've only ever seen one intaglio ring of Laverna."

"On whom?" I say, and the moment lengthens between us, laden with the unspoken.

Then he says quietly, "On Virgil Thorne."

I can't contain my disbelief. "Her father? Are you sure?"

He nods. "It's his ring. You see, when he first acquired it, the stone had a noticeable chip. He repaired it himself with gold—a controversial decision. It's an old Japanese art called kintsugi, devised to fix broken pottery. A special lacquer of powdered gold, silver, or platinum is poured into the crack, giving the piece a unique appearance. I saw that very repair on the ring. It's unmistakable."

I look down at the glove crunched in my hand. Everything darkens around me.

"Mr. Curtis, you mustn't give up," Luke says, and I hear the urgency in his words. "If that man has done something to Mr. Thorne, you must apprehend him."

"When did you last see or speak to Virgil Thorne?" I ask hoarsely.

"Not for several years, I'm afraid. When he was obliged to retire from the company, he was understandably displeased by the way it came about. He had only himself to blame, and he knew it, but Virgil Thorne isn't someone who admits to his flaws. You don't succeed in our business by diffidence. He succeeded because of who he is: a man of intense ambition, passion, and considerable charm. Much like Ania." Luke's voice softens. "She'll be devastated should something untoward befall him. She's always worshiped him, as he worships her. She's his only child. Do what you must, but do it quickly. Find this thief. He has Virgil Thorne's ring and that can't be a good sign."

"No," I say, swallowing against the horrible sensation in my chest as I shove the glove into the pocket of my jeans. "Not good at all."

At that moment, Ania returns. She pauses in the doorway to regard us, but if she senses the tension, the echo of a revelation that could shatter what remains of her world, she doesn't make an indication of it. I'm as disconcerted as much by her cool demeanor as by what I've just heard. But I push the revelation inside me so it doesn't advertise itself on my face, saying instead to Luke, "Take care now. Get better soon."

He laughs. "I intend to. One night in this antiseptic excuse for a room is all I'll bear."

Ania says in her cut-crystal voice, "Are you ready, Mr. Curtis?"

I nod.

She gives Luke a smile. "Henri's in recovery. I'm assured his injuries aren't severe, but he must stay here for at least a week, so be glad you only have to endure one night."

"You should give that man a raise," Luke says. "He's earned it."

His cavalier tone shouldn't surprise me; like her, Luke Westerly has apparently learned to master his emotions. Whatever happens, nothing seems to disturb his louche-gentleman-about-town air.

Must be a jewelry thing, I think as we say goodbye, Ania promising to telephone later to check in. At the hospital exit, I tell her, "Wait here. I'll bring the car around."

"To the bank," she says as soon as she gets into the front seat, the bag planted on the floorboard between her feet.

"Right," I say.

But as I follow her directions, I can't stop thinking about how I have to tell her that the father whom she worships may have been kidnapped—or worse—by the very thief who stole her jewelry and just gave chase after us.

Or, I think with a cold drop in my belly, *that he might be the Leopard himself.*

Chapter Ten

Ania

Jerome insists on parking two blocks from the bank, close to a busy taxi stand.

"What are you doing?" I ask him.

"He saw our car earlier. Passed right by us. He'll know soon enough, if he doesn't already, there's nothing in those cases he wants. He accosted Darcy outside your bank and could be watching to see if we arrive here. We'll leave the car and take a taxi to the bank. But first—" He turns to me. "Do you have a scarf in that bag to put over your head, to hide your hair so if he is watching, we can increase our chances of getting into the bank without him trying to intercept us?"

"Don't you have a gun?" I retort. "I'm done with the pantomime—" I stop myself. I'm angry at him for failing to catch the thief, but he didn't cause the accident, and he's been right about everything else so far. The Leopard, if that's even who he is, is clearly after me, or what I have, so I can't assume he isn't preparing another unexpected attack.

I search in my bag and locate a dark blue sweater. I change into it, then remove one of my father's diamond bracelets from a black and gold Hermès scarf, wrapping the bracelet in my soiled blouse. Folding the silk scarf into a triangle, I fasten it under my chin and tuck my chignon under it. "Satisfied?" I put on my sunglasses. "Do I look like an ordinary Parisian woman on her way to the bank?"

Jerome nods. No quip or comment. This change that's come over us is unsettling, though I initiated it. From strangers to lovers to strangers again, except now we're also like wary soldiers, hampered by our inability to stave off the unseen enemy.

The next part goes smoothly enough, though my heart hammers in my chest. From the car to the nearest taxi. From the taxi, the swift walk to the bank, Jerome's hand inside his jacket at his holster.

"I'll wait here," he tells me in the bank entryway.

A security guard at the entry eyes us because we're acting suspiciously, until I inform him in French that the man is my bodyguard, and I'm here to make a deposit in my vault. That I need to see the manager, Monsieur Allard. Only valued clients would ask for M. Allard by name, so the guard assents, giving Jerome impassive side-eye.

"Shall I tell him someone could be following us?" I ask Jerome.

"Why?" he says. "He's not going to steal from the bank, I already told you that." There's a sharpness in his voice that rouses my anger again.

"Fine," I retort and make my way through the richly decorated marble lobby, into the bank, and to M. Allard's office.

It takes only a few minutes to fill out the necessary paperwork required to be taken into the dungeon, as my father dubbed the subterranean vault, which according to legend was once the oubliette of a long-demolished château that once occupied this parcel of land.

"I hope your visit to Paris is going satisfactorily, Mademoiselle Thorne," M. Allard says politely as he escorts me past the imposing gates leading down the staircase to the impressive thick steel-plated door that allows entry to the vault.

I nod. "Yes, as always," I say, wondering if he's already heard of the theft in Cannes. If it's splashed across every newspaper, it means he's fully aware of the enormous loss I've incurred. He would never mention it, being who he is, but if he knows, then I hope he takes extra precautions with what I'm about to deposit.

He leans down to Box 516, one of the largest on the bottom row. He puts his key in into the first lock. I hand him my personal key for the second lock. And then he opens the door to the fireproof cabinet where my father has safeguarded our jewels for years while in Paris.

"Can I be of further assistance?" he asks.

"No, thank you. This will only take a few minutes."

"Please call when you're ready." He indicates the telephone on the wall.

I move my bag onto the table.

I feel as if I'm about to conduct a religious service, removing these precious objects that I could have lost just hours ago, now hiding them for safekeeping. Protecting them from the criminal at my heels, waiting for the opportunity to deprive me of my legacy.

I unwrap each piece from the assortment of underwear, scarves, stockings, and blouses. Then I realize I can't just put all the jewels into the box without any protection. The insides of the case linings are designed to be removed, so the jewels can be easily moved into this cabinet, and I was taught how to care for the jewelry before I was ever allowed to touch it. I've never put a single piece away without first securing it within its satin-lined container.

I'm at a loss. Another of those unexpected moments, of which I've had too many in the last twenty-four hours, that test my mettle and sunder my heart. There are traditions. Rules. Protocols. There are memories. And I'm sacrificing every one because of some lunatic who evidently has it out for my company and me.

All of a sudden, a bitter laugh bursts from my lips. An ugly sound that isn't like me at all.

I reach for the phone. "M. Allard," I say when he answers. "I do need some help, after all. Can you send down a dozen large envelopes and a box of facial tissues?"

He doesn't ask why. He arrives within minutes with the requested items and retreats without a word of inquiry.

Carefully, I wrap each piece in tissue, padding them, and then place each in its own envelope. It takes me about twenty minutes to finish storing the jewelry, return my clothes to my bag, call M. Allard, and depart the bank. Relief overwhelms me; I feel limp. Exhausted, in fact. With the jewels now safe in the vault, the events of the last forty-eight hours fall upon me like inescapable jet lag, leaving me in a haze and in urgent need of absolute privacy, like what I experience after I finish designing a collection.

I have nothing left to give. I need to replenish myself.

Jerome is smoking outside. He takes me by my arm and leads me like a child toward the rental car. I notice he's keeping his eye on the windows of every establishment we pass.

"What are you looking at?" I ask, though I know I probably

shouldn't. It's done. The jewels are safe. If nothing else, at least we've prevented another calamity.

"Reflections in the glass," he says. "Easiest way to see if we're being followed."

"Are we?"

"So far, no."

We don't say another word until we're in the car.

"I want to go to my apartment," I tell him, and before he can respond, I direct him to turn left on Avenue George V and continue onto Pont de l'Alma. I love the bridge and have walked across it often, but this time there's no joy in it, no pleasure from the gorgeous view, the way the sunlight glitters on the Seine as we cross the river and turn left onto Quai d'Orsay. From Boulevard Saint-Germain, I tell Jerome to turn left onto Rue du Bac. This is my neighborhood, and I feel the tightness in my body loosen. I know the baker on the corner, the florist next to him. I've always shopped at the wine store down the block, purchased groceries from the store run by generations of the same family. Though it's foolish of me, I always feel as if nothing bad can happen to me here.

We turn left onto Rue de l'Université.

"Number 50," I say.

"Okay." As he slows down to look for a space, he says, "Ania, we need to talk."

"Yes, I know." I'm not sure if I'm relieved or troubled that he's finally breached the tension between us. "But must we do it now? I'm so tired. I don't feel like—"

"Yes. Now. As soon as we get into your apartment." His tone is serious.

Once he's parked, we head into my building. My apartment is on the third floor, and I take the stairs, ignoring his offer to carry my bag. The elevator is too slow, and I love climbing the staircase with its zebra wood-paneled walls and balustrade, designed by Edgar Brandt, the famous wrought-iron designer. He was just one of the artisans who worked on this building; when it first opened, it was hailed as one of the finest examples of Paris's Art Deco style. Stunning in its geometric lines and subtle use of color; never sentimental, Art Deco represents everything modern, luxurious, and progressive.

Like so much of my father's work.

I unlock the apartment door and almost let out a cry to finally be in a place I call home. As I dump my bag onto the sofa, I hear him say in surprise, "This belongs to you?"

"To my family." I glance at him. "Why?"

"It's…impressive. I thought Paris apartments were supposed to be small."

"It is small. Two bedrooms. It belonged to Naomi Blanc, who designed Chanel's costume jewelry. She was my godmother. I spent summers apprenticing with her from the time I was fourteen until I turned nineteen, the year my mother died. Naomi was very dear to me." I hear myself saying this as if it's of vital importance that he understands, and I know I'm just evading what I sense coming. If I fill the silence and chatter on about things he doesn't care about, maybe I can forestall the calamity looming between us.

I show Jerome into the living room that looks out onto an internal courtyard, planted with trees and the ivy that has crawled up past my windows to the rooftop.

"I'll make some coffee. Then we can discuss what we need to."

"Yeah, coffee sounds good." He looks uncomfortable, as if he's not sure what to do with himself.

"You can smoke on the balcony," I tell him, and I go into the kitchen to start the espresso pot. I busy myself, forcing away any thoughts of what's happened. I just need to get through this conversation with Jerome and see him out so I can be alone. I'll offer to pay for his hotel room. But I need time to myself, to figure out what I'm going to do next.

I bring out a tray with the coffee, a bowl of sugar, and a plate of stale biscuits I scavenged in the cabinet. "Sorry, no milk. I haven't had time to contact my housekeeper to stock the kitchen. I was here for one night when I arrived from New York, and I ate out."

"I take it without milk or cream," he says.

I've had a very intimate night with this man, and I have no idea how he takes his coffee. I don't know anything about him, really, except what he's told me, but nothing of his personal likes or dislikes, the way he prefers things. Does he use an alarm to get up in the morning? Does he like to read novels or newspapers? What kind of music does he listen to? The kind of things lovers usually learn about each other. But we won't. There's no time for us. Just those few hours when he'd been exactly who I needed him to be and I was…well, I don't know what I've been to him.

Now, I'll never find out.

I sip my coffee, while he puts two heaping teaspoons of sugar in his. I watch him stir. Too many times. He's also delaying. He doesn't want to say whatever he thinks he should.

I sigh. "Jerome. Just go ahead."

He looks up at me. That look in his eyes…

"What is it?" A part of me hopes he's trying to gather the nerve to talk me out of filing the insurance claim. Another part of me hopes, and also dreads, he's trying to figure out how to talk about what's happened between us.

Then he says flatly, "I spoke to Luke at the hospital when you went to see Henri. He had more of an interaction with the Leopard than he told you."

"Oh?" A chill sweeps over me.

"Ania, he saw something." He half rises from the sofa, pulls a crumpled black cloth from his pocket, and sets it on the table between us.

Not a cloth. A glove.

"He tore this off the Leopard as they fought over the cases. Luke saw his hand."

I sit utterly still.

"He was wearing a distinctive ring," I hear Jerome say. "Luke recognized it. He thinks your father might be in danger."

"My father?" It's the last thing I expect to hear, and I'm taken aback by how calm I sound. "How?"

"The ring. Luke told me…"

I can't move. I can't even put down the coffee cup in my hands as I meet his stare.

"Luke said the ring belongs to your father," Jerome says.

"That's impossible," I whisper.

"It had a design. An intaglio, Luke called it. Of a Roman goddess. Repaired with gold."

I see the ring in my mind as if it's on the table by the glove. I know it so well. I was fascinated by it as a child. My father explained how he repaired it. *"The old made new again,"* he'd said. He's always worn it with pride. As long as I've known him, he's never taken it off. It's so integral to him, like an inseparable part of his being.

"Intaglios are common," I say, even as a chasm opens inside me. "Luke was fighting for his life. He suffered a head wound. He must have been mistaken. It could have been a signet ring that looked like an intaglio in the confusion."

"Would Luke make that kind of mistake?"

"You said it yourself. It happened so fast. Luke's very observant; it's why he's so valued. But the accident, the attack…" My voice drifts off. I know from years of working with him that Luke would never make this kind of error. There's no way he could have mistaken that black onyx ring with its gold-filled crack; like me, he's seen it on my father's hand too many times. Besides, I think, even as I try to fight back the thought, what are the odds that the man who stole my jewels would wear a ring so similar to my father's?

"Ania." Jerome's voice wrenches my eyes to him. "When was the last time you spoke to your father?"

"I called him a few days ago. Before I left for Cannes." *Why am I lying to him?*

"And? Where was he?"

"At home." Though I hear the exasperation in my reply, I can't control it. "In New York. Our family home is there. Where else would he be?"

"Huh. Maybe you should call again and make sure." He's looking at me as if he can see the falsehood coursing under my skin. Those x-ray eyes of his that miss nothing.

"But," he goes on, "before you do, I want you to think very carefully about how all of this went down. How the Leopard managed to infiltrate your company by blackmailing an employee. How he knew you'd given the codes of the cases to your assistant. How he's anticipated your every move. How he's stayed so far ahead of us."

"And?" I return his stare. I want to look away but force myself not to. I know where he's heading and it's making me sick, but I refuse to show it. "Your point is…?"

"What do you think my point is?" His voice turns impatient. "We have to consider the possibility that your father is involved. That he might be the Leopard."

I can't speak for an endless moment. I don't look away, and he doesn't either. Not even when I finally say, in a voice so sharp it's like a shard in my mouth, "That's absurd."

"Is it?"

"Yes." I rise to my feet. It's abrupt, unplanned. I should remain seated. Composed. Dismiss his lunacy with the indifference it deserves.

Instead, I hear my voice trembling in rage. "My father is the most famous jeweler in America. One of the most famous jewelers in the world. Are you telling me you think he's a common thief? A *murderer?*"

"I'm telling you the common thief and murderer has his ring."

"Then something must have happened to him!" My voice shatters. "He could be in danger right now, and you—you're here, daring to accuse him of— No." I turn away from him, the apartment tilting around me like a sinking ship. "Please go. Now."

He comes up behind me. "Not until I'm sure you're safe."

"Safe? That's the last thing I am! You were supposed to help me, to find out who's done this, and now you want me to consider that my father stole from other jewelers. Killed a woman over a handful of diamonds, when he has dozens at his disposal. That he stole from his own company. From me. His daughter. That he assaulted Luke and put my life in danger. You want to be sure I'm safe? *How* am I supposed to answer that?"

"Ania." I feel his hands on my shoulders and whirl around to him, my own hand raised. "Don't. I told you, I want you to leave."

"Call New York," he says quietly. "If I'm wrong, you can throw me out."

"I'll do no such thing. You will leave my apartment at once. This is insane. You've cooked up this theory to justify your blunders. Are you really that desperate to catch the Leopard that you'll go so far as to accuse an innocent man?"

"If he's innocent, I'll apologize. Call New York."

I march to the phone. Pick it up and pause. "If you don't mind, I'd like some privacy."

"I'll go buy some cigarettes. Ten minutes. Then I'll be back. I don't want to waste my time or yours, Ania."

I hold my breath until I hear the door close and then I dial the operator, asking her to connect me to my father's penthouse. It rings several times. I'm starting to feel the panic now, the rising fear that my father has been abducted, maimed or killed, his finger severed to get the ring. Already, the Leopard's elaborate scheme to shift the blame onto one of his many victims starts weaving itself in my mind. He's done this to frame us. To frame my father. God, please. Not my father. Anything but—

"Thorne Residence. Hello?"

Gerard. I actually have to grip hold of the sofa edge as I say, "Gerard, I…I'm in Paris. I have to extend my time in Europe."

His voice is gentle. "I know. I read about it today. It's in all the newspapers. Ania, I'm so sorry. You must be devastated."

"I can't afford to be devastated right now. Gerard, I need to speak to my father. Has he already left London? Can you give me the number of his hotel in Barcelona?"

A pause. "He did leave London, but he's not in Barcelona. I spoke to him this morning. He decided to cut short his trip and return here. He saw the headlines."

He's alive. Unharmed. I feel my knees threaten to buckle.

"And he's fine?" I sag against the sofa.

"As far as I know. He's upset by the news, of course. It's why he decided to not continue with his vacation. Why do you ask? Ania, is everything all right?"

I have to sit down. I'm going to collapse. "What time did you speak to him?"

"About eight or so hours ago. It's late here, Ania. The time difference… Did something else happen? You don't sound at all like yourself."

"Yes. I mean, no—"

"Can I do anything?"

"If Papa calls you again…" I'm not sure what else to say. He's on a plane on his way to New York. Why would he call Gerard again? I can't believe I'm even entertaining this suspicion… "Thanks, Gerard. I'm sorry to have woken you."

"Not at all. I was still up reading. I'll tell Mr. Thorne to call you as soon as he arrives. I'm sure he'll want to speak to you, too."

"Yes, thank you. Good night." I hang up and press my hand to my mouth. No. It's not possible. It can't be. But he hasn't tried to contact me here. He hasn't reached out to me, though he's seen the headlines. Though he must know where I am. Where I was. Why hasn't he offered to help me? Why would he fly directly back to New York when he was already in Europe, in London, just a few hours' flight from me?

I dial my uncle Michael in London. The same maid picks up. "I'm afraid not, Miss Thorne. Sir Michael and Lady Agnes left for their country estate. Can I assist in any way?"

"My father was just visiting them. I'm trying to reach him. It's important."

"Oh, yes. Such a delightful gentleman, if you don't mind my saying so. But I'm afraid he left us earlier than expected."

"When did he leave?"

"Oh. Must have been three days ago. He said he had an urgent matter."

Urgent matter…

"Did he say where he was going?"

"Not to me. Why don't you ring Sir Michael at Lakeworth Manor? I have the number here. Oh, wait. They're dining tonight at another estate. Tomorrow, perhaps?"

"Yes," I say faintly. "Tomorrow."

Someone is knocking at the door. Jerome. He's back.

"Miss Thorne, are you still there?"

"Yes. Excuse me. Someone's at my door. Thank you, I'll be in touch."

"Very well. Good day."

I hang up, go to the door, and let him in.

"Well?" He smells of smoke. And he looks haggard. As exhausted as I feel. I can see how much this is affecting him, but I don't want to see it. I don't want to feel any sympathy for him. I can't afford it. Not now.

"My father…" I have to speak slowly. I cannot cry. I can't let him see the despair that threatens to overwhelm me. "He was in London, visiting my aunt and uncle. He was due to leave for Barcelona but decided to return to New York instead."

"He's been in London the entire time?"

"I can give you my uncle's number if you want to verify it. Though I don't think that's necessary. Is it?" Before he can reply, I add, "I've also been called back to New York. The board is very concerned. They want to speak to me about the situation. You should return to London and file our claim."

"When are you leaving? Surely, we have some time to—"

I cut him off. "I'll stay here overnight and leave first thing tomorrow."

"And you're certain this is what you want?" He's not going to try and convince me otherwise. I should be relieved. Why am I not relieved?

"I see no other solution. Do you?"

He goes silent for a moment. "I could go to New York with you."

"That won't be necessary." I extend my hand. "Thank you for all your assistance."

He glances at my hand between us, and I think he's about to smile. Instead, he nods, shoves his hands into his pockets. "I need that glove. For evidence. Then I'll see myself out."

As he retrieves the glove and returns to the door, my voice catches in my throat.

"Jerome."

He pauses, looks over his shoulder at me. Those eyes…

"I'm sorry," I whisper.

"Why? I'm not." He opens the door and leaves me standing there. I listen to the echo of his footsteps fading as he descends the stairs and feel the sudden, desperate urge to call him back. To tell him everything.

Instead, I go to the phone to call the airport. "Please have my jet fueled and readied. I'm leaving for New York. As soon as possible."

Chapter Eleven

Jerome

I can't feel myself moving as I leave her building and start walking towards the parked car down the street. I can't hear the city around me, the inevitable racket of vehicles and people chattering in sidewalk cafés, though this area looks pretty exclusive, mostly residential, and there probably isn't much noise at any time of the day.

Still, I am…shell-shocked. Like when a bomb would fall close during the war and we'd crouch, ears gone numb, packed with nothing, devoid of sound as the earth rocked under our feet. After it stopped, and the ringing in our ears began, we'd hear that percussive blast for hours later. Days. It kept repeating in our heads like an inescapable nightmare. Some of the guys eventually went crazy from the fear and started shooting at any unexpected sound, blasts of friendly fire. Others just went crazy and shut down.

That's what I feel like now. As if an earth-shaking blow has emptied me of sensation, left me adrift in my body, the world around me an indistinct haze.

I should have expected it. I knew the risk. Goddesses don't fall in love with mortals. They use and discard them. Someone like her, with someone like me: what are the odds?

But now I know what it's like to be with her. To feel her hunger, her secret desire to lose herself, even if she tries to deny it. She wasn't pretending with me. She liked it. She took pleasure in it. She showed a side of herself that was pliant and vulnerable. Irresistible. A side I would swear she rarely, if ever, shows to anyone.

I need to get a grip. She's still way out of my league. I should be grateful I had one night and call it like it is. The girl had an appetite, and I fit the menu. She told me, no promises. No expectations. The only expectation she had was that I recover her jewelry.

And I didn't.

I pause by the car, crunching the cigarettes in my coat pocket. What now? I'll have to return the vehicle, I suppose. Itemize it on my expense report, though how I'm going to explain a rental car in Paris will be something else. Lambert Securities has given me ample leeway thus far, trusting my judgment. I've solved several of their high-profile cases without the rampant publicity they detest, as no insurance firm wants news of a heist splashed across the front page. I've even recovered stolen property and seen it returned with a minimum of extracurricular fuss.

But the Leopard…they don't really know about my obsession with him. Sure, they've let me peruse unsolved case files I think might be connected, even entertained my theories about his penchant for snatch-and-flee with headlines in tow, but they have no idea how much time and effort I've devoted to him, to creating a profile I can anticipate and pursue. They're not an international crime unit. They don't like it when thieves get away and raise the premiums, but they're not in the police business. If I catch one in the process of investigating a claim, kudos to me. One less bad guy to worry about. But to hunt him over the years, with a fervor that precludes my professional obligations…

If I admit I believe he was responsible for this particular theft, that he was within my grasp and I messed up, putting the client I was supposed to assist in danger, to boot—yeah, that won't go well. They'll be disappointed enough to hear the client wishes to file her claim and I better make damn sure they don't ask any more questions. I should cover the rental car myself, take my open-ended plane ticket and go back to London. To my little flat that reeks of stale tobacco smoke and greasy take-out. To my uninvolved and uncomplicated life, with a few drinks at the pub after hours and the occasional waitress to satisfy my infrequent urge for company.

And forget Ania Thorne. Even if I know I can't.

I close my eyes for a moment, willing myself to unlock the car door. I see her instead, extending her long hand with its oddly blunt fingernails, her implacable resolve followed by the whispered apology.

She's sorry. Great. Sorry for what? For being a class-A bitch and tossing me out on my rump because I did a lousy job and then had the audacity to accuse her father of grand larceny? Or sorry that she took me to bed in a moment of weakness only to discover, in the cold light of day beside a crashed car, that she made a mistake?

Yet…there was something else. Something which in the shock of the moment, I'd failed to fully take in. I know she's got that diamond dust in her veins. Cold as a glacier when the mood overtakes her. But there was also fear. I'd seen it before in her, at the hotel in Cannes, and later, at the Ritz; this time, it was different somehow. Not the fear of being robbed again. Of losing her precious reputation or control over her company.

No. Not just fear. Terror. A frantic need to escape what was right in front of her. The question is, why? She called New York. Claims Daddy was right where he was supposed to be. She's going home to address her board's concerns and no doubt, seek shelter in the family home until the storm blows over, leaving her to pick up the pieces.

She'll be devastated should something untoward befall him. She's always worshiped him, as he worships her. She's his only child…

My eyes jolt open. Turning on my heels, I nearly run straight into a passing car. It blares its horn at me. The driver flips his middle finger for emphasis. Guess "watch where you're going, jerk" works in any language. I start racing back to her building, then draw myself up short.

What am I going to say? *Look here, Miss Winner of the Ice Queen Award, I'm not going anywhere. You know what I suggested might be true, so I'm going with you to New York, whether you like it or not, and talk to Daddy myself. I'll risk my job—hell, I can say goodbye to my job when Lambert learns I confronted Virgil Thorne—but until I know for certain he's been holed up in his penthouse the entire time he should have been, with that famous rare ring still on his finger and can provide a list of reliable alibis to back him up for his mysterious short-lived vacation, I'm not taking any chances. Not with you.*

Right. She'll love me for that. She'll declare her immense gratitude that I'm such a strong-willed, conscientious man, the kind of man she's always dreamed about, and open her arms. She'll invite me to question her father about being the most notorious jewel thief of the century. Why not?

I start to turn back to the car. This is insane. She's right. I've lost my marbles. A whiff of Madison Avenue glamour, and I toss every instinct to the wind. I did my job. Badly, but I did it. I know how the jewels were taken and by whom. I know there wasn't client fraud involved. That's all I'm obliged to do. File her claim and admit defeat. Move on. There'll be other cases to solve. There are always other cases where jewelry is involved.

Her father's daughter, Mr. Curtis. Don't ever forget it.

And what would her father's daughter do? She's not in the habit of depending on anyone, much less in a crisis, and this certainly qualifies as one. So, she had to get rid of the guy who treats her like she's risen from the sea on a pearl shell and already has a bug in my ear about her father. Act like it was pleasant, if overwrought at the end, but now it's over and it's time for us to part ways.

Then take her plane back to New York to deal with it herself.

Because Virgil Thorne's daughter doesn't share her problems with others. Virgil Thorne raised his daughter to take care of her problems on her own.

I return to the car, wait for a closer parking space to open up. When it does, I whisk the car into it in a flagrant illegal maneuver that earns me another dose of horn blasts and irate middle fingers. Then I sit there, smoking cigarettes until my mouth is parched, as dusk descends and I keep watch, my attention never wavering from her building entryway.

It's already dark when the taxi pulls up. Because her chauffeur is in the hospital, and the company car is in the repair shop. Because it's anonymous. Hundreds of Parisians take taxis to the airport every day. What's one more?

She emerges with her overstuffed bag. No suitcases, so she's in a hurry. She hasn't changed her clothes, either, which is proof enough. Her sunglasses are perched on her head for an inexplicable reason, and she doesn't pause, doesn't look around first to check if someone's lurking nearby, though she's recently evaded a thief on a motorcycle who caused a near-fatal collision and should, at the very least, be a little paranoid he might track her down at her residence. No. She boards that taxi as if she's never coming back, and as it speeds off into the night, I know my instincts haven't failed me, whiff of glamour aside.

I follow her. Ready or not, New York, here we come.

Chapter Twelve

Ania

The sky is a fire opal as dawn breaks over New York. The landing is rough. I'm not surprised. Nothing about this flight—or my life right now—has been smooth. I'm used to turbulence, but what we encountered over the Atlantic was as bad as I've ever flown through. As if nature herself were flinging up obstacles to detain me. I spent most of the mid-hours of the flight strapped into my seat, gripping the armrest and thinking that if my plane went down, it would be the final epic touch on the catastrophe that's overtaken my existence. When the bad weather eventually faded, my slightly green-faced steward came over to offer me champagne, a hot meal, and a warm towel for my face. With Dom Perignon fizzing in my veins, gourmet food in my stomach, and a towel over my eyes, I finally managed to catch some desperately needed sleep.

Finally, the doors open, and I leave the plane, my overnight bag in hand, and sunglasses on. I need to get to the city and our apartment.

I need to see my father.

As I make my way towards the exit, I'm surprised by how empty Idlewild Airport is at six o'clock in the morning. A skycap approaches, and I refuse his offer of service. I start to hurry down the long hallways, shifting my bag from sore shoulder to sore shoulder. I've been carrying it for days. And now, I'm carrying all my doubts and fears with it.

Other than worrying over whether I'd end up at the bottom of the ocean, I've spent every second of the last fifteen hours worrying about what I'll find here. Mile after mile, I replayed the events that transpired since I arrived in Cannes. How many days ago was that? It seems like months. Longer. I can't even recall what a normal day is like, my usual routine, which if always busy and replete with problems to solve, was still predictable. I was never at a loss as to how to deal with things, never not ready or willing to face challenges. Not like now.

Being tossed about on a plane without solid ground under my feet was the perfect metaphor. I don't know who to trust. From my own employees to— No, it can't be true. It simply can't. Luke made a mistake. Even he isn't infallible, and we were transporting Papa's most celebrated jewels, some of which Luke had seen created, catalogued for storage, overseen, and cared for. It's normal—well, not *normal.* Nothing about this is normal—but still, logical for Luke to have mistaken the ring for something it wasn't. To see what wasn't there.

And Jerome doesn't know my father. He doesn't know anything about us, except for whatever he's read in his insurance dossiers. It's logical for him to have assumed the worst, to have taken Luke at his word. I would have done the same in his position.

That's what I keep telling myself.

Despite the hour, I find plenty of cabs waiting outside. In a voice that catches me unawares in its weariness, I give my father's address: "211 Central Park West, please."

The driver nods and pulls out. I'm hoping he won't be talkative, as cabbies tend to be. I can't deal with banal questions about where I'm going or where I've been. *"Nice weather we're having, isn't it?"* Thankfully, he remains silent as we head for Manhattan. It's probably too early in the morning for him, too. I close my eyes and lean against the seat back. For a moment, I let myself forget the reason of my journey and imagine that when I arrive in the apartment, Gerard will be waiting, with his docile voice and smile, ready to make me an espresso.

But, of course, coffee will have to wait if my father is there. He has to be there. I must find out what he knows about the theft. About whether the thief might be wearing some kind of duplicate ring or whether it was Luke's imagination in the uproar of the moment. Because, of course, that's what it has to be. It's one or the other. There's no other explanation. What Jerome implied is horrific. There could be another ring like my father's; any competent jeweler could copy it. A ring, if it exists, doesn't prove anything.

Due to the hour, a drive that often takes forty minutes only takes twenty. Once we come through the Central Park transverse, I look up, the way I always have, to catch my first glimpse of the Beresford. Home. Even though I have apartments in Los Angeles and in Paris, the storied 1929 skyscraper where I grew up, where so much of who I am began, still remains *home*.

The sun has risen, turning the high clouds pearlescent; it glints off the building's three distinctive octagonal copper-capped towers. My father lives in one of them. Three bedrooms, four bathrooms on the twenty-first and twenty-second floors, with a rooftop terrace overlooking the park. He bought it years ago after his first store opened and became a success. It's worth twice what he paid at the time. To him, it's always been his refuge from the demands of business. Demands I now know too well.

If I prayed, I'd be saying a prayer that he's safely asleep in his bedroom or maybe already up, doing his morning exercises as Gerard prepares breakfast. Papa was always an early riser, and exercising has been a lifetime habit. "Keeping the body fit, tuned like an engine," he'd tell me, "is as important as polishing a gemstone. To burnish out the minor flaws. To encourage the luster, the brilliance within. To exalt the very best in it."

We arrive. As I pay the driver. Robert, our doorman, who's been on guard since I was a little girl and never seems to age, opens the door with his impeccable white gloves.

Seeing me, he smiles. "Welcome home, Miss Thorne."

I climb out of the cab with my bag. Robert reaches for it, but I hold tight. He looks slightly offended. The doorman always offers, and we always let him take our luggage and packages from the car to the elevator, but I haven't had this bag out of my sight since I left Paris and I'm not about to now.

"It's just an overnight bag," I say, forcing out a smile. He nods and goes ahead to open the big brass doors with their glass insets. As I step into the rarefied air of the prestigious building, I feel myself gnawing at my lower lip.

Now that I'm actually here, I almost wish I wasn't.

I start to ask Robert if he's seen my father, but he comes on duty at five a.m., and according to my conversation with Gerard, my father was expected back late last night. It's unlikely Robert saw him arrive.

Teddy, the elevator man, who's been at the Beresford even longer than Robert, starts to rush over to help with my bag. I again decline politely and follow Teddy into the wood and brass cage. He pulls the iron gate shut, and we begin our journey upwards. I count the floors as they light up on the shining brass panel overhead.

Eleven. Twelve.

What am I heading to?

Fifteen.

What am I going to discover?

Eighteen.

We reach the twenty-first floor, and I step off the elevator, then walk to the only door in the hallway. I took out my key on the ride up, but now I think I'll startle Gerard if I use it this early when he's not expecting me. Given the amount of jewelry that's gone in and out of the apartment over the years, Gerard keeps a gun handy. I've never seen it and have no idea where it is, but I assume he keeps it locked away for safety reasons. Gerard is meticulous like that.

I ring the doorbell and wait.

Our butler answers in less than two minutes. The surprise on his face is genuine, as is his greeting. He's still in his dressing gown.

"Ania! I didn't know you were coming home. You didn't say yesterday."

"I didn't know," I say, hearing the disconnected timbre in my voice as if I'm still thousands of miles away on another continent. "Is Papa here?"

"I'm afraid I don't know. He hadn't arrived by the time I went to bed last night, and I haven't seen him yet this morning. I was just going to check upstairs."

"Well, no need. I'll go. You don't have to announce me. I want it to be a surprise," I say with forced lightness. "He's probably still asleep if he arrived that late and we don't want to wake him. You know how grumpy he can be after a long day of travel."

"Yes, of course," Gerard says. "Shall I start the coffee? Are you hungry?"

"A little. I ate on the plane. Coffee would be nice. Espresso." I hear my words and marvel at the normality in them, like it's just another unexpected visit home, an impulsive decision to return to the nest. Like nothing has happened, nothing at all.

In the guest powder room, I take in my appearance. I've never looked quite this bedraggled. I didn't even shower or change my clothes before leaving Paris. If Papa is here, he'll notice. He always took a keen interest in my appearance. Another of his wisdoms imparted to me: "Always look as if you're as prepared to meet them head-on in the boardroom or have drinks at a client's soiree. Never be caught with your guard down."

It doesn't matter. Who cares what I look like? I don't want to waste time on the superficial, but I can't curb the impulse ingrained in me. If I walk into my father's bedroom like this and he's already awake, he'll know something isn't right at once.

I don't want that to happen.

Taking my makeup bag, I re-apply lipstick, blot my nose with powder, then brush out and re-knot my hair. I dab on some perfume from the little bottle of L'Etoile's *Noir.*

Done. I fasten my Hermès scarf around my neck—a trick my French mother taught me. "A bit of colored silk hides a multitude of sins," she used to say.

Back in the hallway, I head in the opposite direction to the sweeping staircase that leads to the living quarters on the penthouse's top floor.

One. Two.

I've always counted the twenty-five steps as I climb them and find myself falling into the pattern. My mother used to count them, too. I lost her when I was sixteen and have lived nearly half my life without her. I'm not ready to lose my father. I shiver at the thought.

Four. Five.

When Jerome showed me the glove and cited the ring—I didn't want to believe my father might have been kidnapped. Or worse. But then Gerard told me he'd spoken to him. That Papa was headed back home. He had to be alive. Safe. Not even the Leopard could abduct a man at Heathrow, cut off his finger to take a ring, and make it back to Paris in time.

Ten.

I went over and over the timeline on the plane. When exactly had my father left London? When did he call Gerard? What if my father had already been abducted and held at gunpoint, forced to call home and feign his return? Is he even here?

Twelve. Thirteen. Fourteen.

What if he isn't? What will I do next? Call the police and report his kidnapping? Wait by the phone until I receive his finger in a box with another cryptic note?

Sixteen.

But something inside me, an infallible feeling as familiar to me as the home around me, and as unsettling as the moment when the motorcycle roared past me, tells me he's here. Jerome could be right. The intimacy of the crime in Cannes, the hunt for the replacements, the brutality of the attack on Luke… Only someone with inner knowledge of how our company operates, and the people involved, could have set in motion those events. Who else but my father would have known to blackmail a specific employee I'd hired after his retirement or been aware of the minute details of my schedule, or surmised how I'd react to the note with the returned necklace? Who else would have assumed I'd already sent for replacements?

As much as I resist it, as much as I don't want to believe it, I can't deny the possibility.

Eighteen. Nineteen.

And if it is true, what will happen to the company? To us? I feel like my mind is breaking apart. The theft has plunged Thorne & Company into chaos we've never experienced before. I have only a shred of a chance of saving it, if the jewels are never recovered. I can't assume the board will elect to keep me at the helm. I can't assume the insurance claim will go through or we'll surmount the headlines. When a jeweler gets hit like this, in such a spectacular way, it creates a ripple effect. Reporters go on a rampage, eager to milk every last drop of publicity. Suppliers hike up their prices. Clients murmur their regrets and seek less tainted options, especially if the thief is the Leopard. He's gone after private collections, too; stolen invaluable pieces from women's bedrooms. And if my father is the Leopard, any chance of saving the company will be lost. We'll be doomed.

I can't let that happen. No matter what I find out, I must contain it, keep the board and the press from ever learning the truth. I'll have to put everything I love on the line to ensure my company survives it.

Twenty-two. Twenty-three. Twenty-four.

The landing.

To the right is my childhood bedroom. I glance at the closed door. When my father traveled, as he often did, I had trouble sleeping. My mother would read to me until I drifted off. I can picture her now. And I can see my shelves of art supplies bought by my father to hone my drawing and designing skills, preparing me for a career at his side.

No. I can't think about any of that now.

I turn left towards my father's study. The door is open, but it's dark inside. And empty. I continue down the hall to my parent's suite, which includes a bedroom, bathroom, and large walk-in closets. This door is shut. Should I knock? I do so, softly. Listen. Hear no response. I put my hand on the knob and turn it slowly, terrified now of what might lie before me.

I step inside. The bedroom looks empty. The lights dim. The heavy peach-colored drapes are still drawn against the daylight, the light beige carpet almost white, like a sea of mist. The bed is made; it hasn't been slept in.

My breath stalls in my throat.

He's not here. Where is he? Is he hurt somewhere? Under duress? Worse?

Then I notice the bathroom door is ajar. The light is on. I glance over at the closets and see my mother's side wide open.

Why would her closet be open?

I move toward it as if in a trance. Is that a shadow inside? At the threshold, I stop, reaching for the doorframe. The scent of my mother's Shalimar overwhelms me. She's been gone so long, but her perfume never evaporates. It lingers, resurrects her memory with acute vividness. All her clothes are here, stored in garment bags. No one had the heart to dispose of them. No one has unzipped the bags to touch the gorgeous silks, the velvets, the fine wools or exotic furs. As if she's gone off on an errand and will return at any moment.

But as I force myself to step inside, I hear a slight crunch and look down. A garment bag has fallen off the rail, now crumpled on the floor. It feels like such a desecration that I almost pull back. Turn my head to look behind me. Then I see the other garment bags tossed upon the bed as if someone has been rummaging in the closet.

I move forward. At the end, which contains a wall of shelves for her shoes, there's a gap. The wall is open like a door to reveal a space behind it that I never knew existed.

And there, in that space, I find my father. Leaning forward and rifling through a safe. At his feet is a valise. And it's full of…leather jewel cases. Not Thorne cases. Others. The red and green and black leathers of our competitors. The gilded insignias of a dizzying array of the best jewelers in the world.

As I see this, as it rushes upon me with the force of a tidal wave, I hear Jerome listing those names in my mind. All the jewelers hit by the Leopard. His unsolved heists.

Every one of them.

"Papa?"

He turns. In his left hand, he clutches a handful of passports.

I don't know how to react. What to say. In my confusion, what comes out is a plaintive: "What are you doing?"

Of all the things I might say, I say that?

"My princess, you're home. How wonderful," he says as if it's no surprise to him. As if I've come upon him in his armchair, reading *The Times* and sipping his morning coffee. But he's not. We are in my deceased mother's closet.

"I thought you might have been kidnapped," I blurt out.

"Kidnapped?" He chuckles, that warm rumble from deep within his chest.

"Haven't you heard? There was an accident. In Paris. Our replacements. The thief tried to get them. Luke—he was injured. Henri, too. Luke saw a ring on the thief's hand…" As I stammer, I feel myself narrowing inside, focusing on his face to gauge his reaction. I see only dismay, followed by immediate paternal concern.

"Are you okay? How is Luke? An accident. How awful."

"Yes, I'm…" I hesitate. This can't be real. "Papa, don't you understand? This thief…the one they call the Leopard. He stole my collection in Cannes. They—Jerome, I mean—he thinks the thief is after me. That it's personal."

"And you think he abducted me, too? That's why you're here?" A sudden grin, a flash of practiced charm, like a film star at a premiere. "My poor Ania. I hate that you were so worried about me. As you can see, I'm perfectly fine."

I can't even speak. I look at his hand wrapped around the passports, at the ring circling his index finger. His intaglio. My thoughts ricochet, exploding inside me. My father is here. He has his ring. A handful of international passports. Packing up jewel cases from every firm robbed by the Leopard. In my mother's closet, before a secret vault.

How can this be happening? How can he act as if he's happy to see me, concerned for me? All the evidence is here. Undeniable. It's all true.

Jerome was right.

My voice hardens. "I was in the car behind Luke. Did you know that?"

He sighs. "That was unfortunate. I never meant to put you in serious harm's way. I didn't anticipate it could all go so…wrong. Entirely my responsibility, of course. I got careless."

"Careless?" I echo, my voice rising in horror. "I don't understand. You—you did this? Why? Why would you steal from our competitors? From their clients? From *me*? Why, Papa? Give me an explanation I can understand for all of this."

He regards me without a change in his expression. Only now, even as the tidal wave bursts inside and shatters my final delusion, my last hope that it's all been a dreadful mistake, I see his expression hasn't changed because he has none. His face is blank, like a mask. An imitation. He looks the same, his silvery hair cropped short to his strong-boned head, his wide cheekbones that age hasn't diminished, his deep-set magnetic eyes and thick eyebrows arched just so, as if he's about to tell a dirty joke. A mask. It's him, yet not him.

"You answered your own question. They were our competitors. Second-rate and soaking up attention. Stealing it from us. All I did was make certain they faltered, lost something. Were taken down a bit. I had to prove we were above them, that no one is better than we are. That no one can ever be."

"But you stole from us in Cannes. From our own company!"

"That was different. I didn't like having to do it."

"Then why?" My voice fractures.

"Why do you think? I had to defend myself, show the board they were wrong to oust me. Yes, I treated some clients poorly—but only the way they deserved to be treated. Just because their name is on a marquee doesn't give them the right to not pay their bill. The vulgarity of fame, thinking it entitles you to do as you please. The clients had to be taught a lesson. The board had to be taught a lesson."

"A *lesson*?" I'm reeling now, the ground yawning like a pit underneath me.

"I built this company from nothing. For you. For us. To give your mother the life she deserved. To give you a legacy to inherit. So we'd never lose what is ours. They took it from me as if I were an inconvenience. An old racehorse past its glory. Put out to pasture. Except for me, it was the slaughterhouse."

"But I took over in your stead," I say helplessly, desperate now for something I can comprehend, something to hold onto. "I'm your daughter. It's still your company."

He stands quiet for a moment, then lets the passports fall into the valise.

"Is it? Because when they turned it over to you, I thought you'd appeal at once. Fight to keep me on. Surely, I deserved that much. But you didn't, did you, my princess? You took charge and thought you could do better. I had no choice."

"Better? You trained me my entire life to take over."

"When I was ready to hand you the reins. Not like this. Not before. They stole my business from me. No one steals from Virgil Thorne."

My gaze lowers to the jewel boxes in the valise.

"I did everything you trained me to do. I did it in our name."

"It's my name, Ania. I gave it to you."

"I thought…you always said you were so proud of me."

"And I am, princess. Your work, your ideas—they're magnificent. You are every bit as talented as I imagined you could be. Why do you think I devoted so much time to you?"

And now my rage bursts forth, blinding me. Not just at my father for what he's done, but for stealing away so much of my youth.

It's as if a cherished illusion has been ripped asunder. All those times he smiled in approval to see me sketching at his library desk, while my mother shook her head, I was only six years old. A little girl, who should have been playing with dolls, not trying to follow in his footsteps, to be the daughter he deserved. And when I turned ten and wanted to go to summer camp he insisted I go to work on the bench at Thorne & Company instead, to learn from his master jewelers. No play dates during school holidays either, because he had design assignments for me, regardless of how much homework I had. As I grew older, what was established in my childhood became the rule by which I had to exist. I must devote my entire life, my heart and soul, to his work. Never once could I recall him asking me if it was what I wanted to do. It never occurred to him that I might not. It never occurred to me. I'd done *everything* he expected, to please him. To be worthy of his praise. Of his love.

"You're punishing me for becoming who you wanted me to be?" I say through my clenched jaw. "For being better than you?"

He looks at me, his smile sincere but his face unmoved. I know he loves me. That's the irony of it. He does. I feel it in the way he reaches out to caress my cheek. How he takes my limp hand and raises it to his mouth, kissing it gently as he's done since I was a girl, always the gentleman who values gallantry in an increasingly crass world. "My princess. I suppose in a way, I am punishing you. But you'll forgive your father his little weakness, won't you?"

I wrench my hand from him. "Weakness? You put everything in danger for your weakness! Our company's reputation. Our employees. *Me.*"

"It was necessary. I had to prove you're not invulnerable. A difficult lesson to learn, isn't it? The last one I have to teach you. There is diamond dust in your veins, but you're not meant to be a solitaire." He bends down to zip up the valise, rises to face me. "My job is done. The board got what they deserved. Thorne & Company can't be successful without its founder, its creator. Without me, there is no company. But in case you think I don't care, I'm leaving your jewels here. The ones you designed for Cannes. Oh, and your shoes, as well." His sudden smile chills me where I stand. "That was quite clever of Luke. His loyalty is to be commended; you don't find his kind of dedication anymore. You must see that he gets a decent raise. Or a suitable retirement, if the company doesn't survive."

From the valise, he removes a sapphire and diamond bangle bracelet, one I designed for Miss Taylor. "There's nothing here worth my effort. Except this." He pauses, with a nostalgia as heartbreaking to me as it is terrifying. "Do you remember when I taught you to braid the stones like this, to create a pattern like cloth? A tapestry of diamonds. This, Ania, is my legacy in you. You can stray from me; design all those newfangled creations everyone thinks are so innovative and daring. But this—this is *ours.* This is what remains of who we were." He returns the bracelet to the valise, moves past me as I stand frozen in place.

"Where...where are you going?" I hear myself whisper.

"I'm not sure. Someplace where I can design again. I have all the raw stock I need." He gestures to the valise in his hand, filled with stolen jewels. "We shall see."

"I should stop you," I say, but I already know I won't. I can't. I'm utterly helpless. Like I'm back on the plane, with nowhere to hide. Buffeted by winds I can't control. What am I supposed to do? Wrestle him to the floor? Yell for help? For Gerard to bring his gun? He's my father and he's a thief. A criminal.

He's still my father.

He takes his jacket from the armchair by the bed and shrugs it on. Then he reaches into its pocket. As he pulls out a suede pouch, something else drops to the floor, but I don't pay attention to it. He opens the pouch, extracts a rope of pearls. My mother's natural, pink-tinged pearl necklace. His gift to her on her thirtieth birthday. It took him five years to find the matching pearls. They gleam the way they always did around her neck. He gave me all of my mother's jewelry when I turned twenty-one, except for those pearls. He said they'd be mine when he died, but he couldn't bear to part with them until then.

He cups them now in his palm, like a pilgrim revering a relic.

I have a sudden memory of my mother at a party in this apartment. I couldn't have been older than twelve. She was standing by the terrace in a wide black cocktail dress, wearing the necklace. Sipping champagne as she watched my father charm one of the fawning female guests. The woman leaned close to Papa, her lipstick too red at his ear, whispering; in that moment, he looked away, over to my mother, and he winked.

She laughed.

My mother didn't know I was watching until I later asked her what was so funny.

"Your father is so charming," she said. "So good at what he does. That woman will be in our shop first thing tomorrow, spending her husband's money on our jewelry. She'll wonder if your father's flirting might lead to something more. She'll hope it will. I laughed because so many women worry their husbands betray them, but with your father, I never need to question it. Virgil Thorne will never love anyone as much as he loves himself."

My father extends the pearls to me. "I believe these belong to you."

I take them from him.

And he leaves me without another word.

Chapter Thirteen

Jerome

By the time my plane lands in Idlewild and I get through customs, pushing my way through hordes of tired passengers and wailing kids trudging toward the luggage area, I'm on the verge of panic.

Ania departed Paris on her plane a few hours before I secured a seat on a commercial flight, which cost more than I anticipated, decimating my dwindling cash. But I'm here. In New York, if still a cab drive from the city, and all I want to do is pee and get going.

In the airport restroom, after I zip up my fly and splash water on my face to wash off some of the grime of nearly sixteen hours of travel, I see myself in the mirror.

God Almighty. I look like crap. I haven't shaved in days, so I practically have a beard, and my eyes are raw, the sleepless nights—I did manage to doze off for a few hours on the plane—and overall lack of hygiene making me look like I crawled out from under a rock. Rummaging in my bag, I locate a comb with missing teeth, a stiff toothbrush, and a dried-out tube of paste. A bottle of my pomade, almost empty, so sadly it won't accomplish much with the rat's nest on my head. My new—well, not so new now—gabardine suit shoved into a bundle at the bottom of my bag, like a soiled mess hall tablecloth.

I packed for a few days in Cannes. I never pack enough, but this… How am I supposed to even get into her building at—Christ, where am I going anyway?

During the overpriced cab drive into Manhattan, I pull out the dossiers, which have fared no better than my comb and toothbrush.

211 Central Park West. The family penthouse. Where Ania was raised, and her mother died. Where Virgil Thorne first established himself as the enterprising son of a Czech immigrant and became a force in the jewelry business, expanding his empire to the glittering realm of Hollywood and ornate palaces of Europe. Reading over his dossier now, knowing what I suspect, I can mark the telltale signs that eluded everyone—including me. His swift climb to the zenith of a perilous industry. His fantastical acquisition of one-of-a-kind stones and unique designs catapulting him to fame, making his company the most recognized and profitable in our field. A celebrity in and of itself, coveted and envied.

Not one lasting setback. Not one serious theft. While his competitors and their clients suffered blow after blow at the Leopard's hands, millions in losses that accumulated and took down a few, leaving Thorne to consolidate his stranglehold—it's right here, in black and white. What first looks like a fairy tale rise to power by a master talent, the proverbial American dream, now reads as a well-orchestrated masterplan, a curse perpetrated by him on others. Curses are an age-old tradition in jewelry, and every theft, every jewel taken, ensured he could step into the curse he created.

None of the stolen property recovered. For a reason. He didn't steal to sell on the black market or dismantle the stones. He stole to enrich his company's value. To keep it on top, toppling every aspirant to his throne.

If it's true. If he is what I think he is.

And she's heading right toward him. Might already be there, confronting a man she adores and admires, whose capacity for deception is equaled only by his ruthless disregard for law or morality. A man capable of murder. Of ripping off his own daughter.

Ania has no idea what awaits her. If it's true.

I urge the cab driver to pick up the pace. Morning rush hour hits us, the avenues of the concrete jungle teeming with cars. The sidewalks crammed with pedestrians hurrying to work. The immense buildings looming like cathedrals of profit. The thunder of America.

The cab pulls up to the address in the exclusive Upper West Side and I pay the fare, hop out, and stand there, staring at its faux-Gothic exterior, one of those turn-of-the-century façades with lavishly discreet adornments to mimic the fantasy of Old Europe.

I shoulder my bag, take stock of my surroundings. There'll be a doorman. An elevator to the penthouse that needs to be made accessible. Questions. Lots of questions. Am I expected? By whom? *"And may I ask, who are you exactly, sir?"*

New York City suspicion. It's endemic here. And in buildings like these, essential.

I avoid my reflection in the glass doors as I make my entrance. I'm going to get into that penthouse, no matter what. I'd just rather not battle a querulous doorman. It won't be easy, but I have to convince him to let me onto the elevator, even if I look like a hobo.

He's portly, dressed in some ridiculous blue-and-gold uniform. Standing behind the marble-fronted lobby desk like every little man with a well-paying job, guarding the domain of those who'll never see him as their equal. Who give him generous tips for walking the poodle on rainy afternoons and decorating the lobby for Christmas. The kind of little man, like M. Saucey at the Carlton, who takes himself too seriously and is immune to bribes.

"Jerome Curtis. To see Ania Thorne." Might as well start with the direct approach.

"Is that so?" He regards me with a Bronx-bred contempt that makes it plain he doesn't believe Miss Thorne can possibly be expecting anyone like me.

"Just call up and ask. I'll wait."

He puffs his lips, picks up the phone. I step aside as if I don't doubt the outcome, even as I strain to overhear. It takes a few seconds. He puts the phone down, rounds the desk, and waddles in his too-tight frockcoat getup to the gilded elevator door.

"This way, sir."

While another self-important toady in a similar costume directs the elevator, I take a deep breath, instinctively reaching under my jacket for the holster that's no longer there. I didn't think boarding an international flight with a gun would be a wise move, so I locked it in the trunk of the rental car in the airport garage. It feels like I'm missing a limb. If it's true, how will I deal with Ania's father if he turns violent?

The elevator door slides open. A hall of padded silence. Even the air feels different here. Muffled. Perfumed somehow, but not by any detectable scent. By the aura of privilege and comfort, of soft-shoed maids and silver platters and not a care in the world.

Or none anyone can see.

I take a step to the only door in the hall. Knock on it.

A bald man in a dressing gown opens it, with the chain-lock still attached. He peers at me through the crack. "Yes? May I help you, sir?"

"I'm here for Ania," I say, and he undoes the chain.

The place is immense, especially to me. My London flat lets me sit on the can and make toast in the kitchen at the same time. It's also quiet. Too quiet. I expect shouting. The furor of long-withheld secrets spilling out like stolen gems. I hear nothing. And it unnerves me to such an extent that when the man behind me says, "I'm the family butler. Gerard. Are you one of her friends?" I whirl to him, reaching again for the gun that isn't there.

My voice is like gravel. "Where is she?"

"Upstairs. In her parents' bedroom." He lets out a small sigh. "She must be distraught. It's down the corridor. All the way. The suite at the end."

"And…him?" I ask.

Gerard the butler takes a moment as if he has to debate the ramifications of betraying his employer's whereabouts. "Gone, I'm afraid."

"Gone?" I move angrily toward him. Stop when I see him flinch. "Where?"

"I don't know. London, perhaps. The villa at Lake Cuomo. He didn't say."

I bolt up the flight of stairs, race down the hallway with its framed portraits without seeing any of it, through large ajar doors and into a spacious and pristine white room that's too dark, garment bags strewn across the bed, and the far closet doors open. The air isn't like downstairs. It's heavy. Too thick. Almost oppressive.

"Ania?" I can't raise my voice. Like an invisible fist is jammed into my sternum. As I turn to the shadows by the bed, to the plush armchair beside it, I see her huddled on it, knees drawn to her chin like a child after a scolding, told to sit quiet until dinner. Or else.

My bag drops from my shoulder.

"Why?" Her eyes are huge. Full of despair. "Why did you tell me? I didn't want to know. I shouldn't have ever known. It's your fault. Because of you, I lost my father."

It takes me a moment before I can pull my voice out of my gut. "He admitted it?"

Her answer is to fling something at me. A black glove.

"He did it for me. For us. He did it to ensure my mother would have the life she deserved. That I'd have a legacy to inherit. That we'd never lose what he fought so hard to build." Her voice is an accusatory hiss. She jabs her hand at the closet. "See for yourself."

Stepping to the closet, treading past a strewn garment bag, I catch sight of the false panel pulled aside, the hidden safe, like a vault in the wall, with a coded lock on the door. Inside, glistening within a black canvas bag, jewelry. Lots of it.

"Is this…?" My voice carries in the silence without an echo, as if the bedroom was designed to be soundproof.

When she doesn't answer, I return to her. She hasn't shifted from the chair, but her posture is coiled now. Taut. Like a panther about to spring, with its fangs bared.

"Is that what I think it is?" I ask.

"Yes. All of it. Everything he took from Cannes." She falters.

"What?" I want to take her in my arms. If anyone needs a hug right now, it's her, but that ferocious expression on her face warns me it won't be welcomed. She's wounded and cornered. Like leopards, panthers strike out when they're in pain.

"He…he kept something for himself. A bracelet."

"Why?"

"Because he…he taught me how to create the pattern with diamonds—" She falters once more. Makes a constricted sound in her throat. "The only piece that reminds him of who we were to each other."

I don't know what to say. I came here anticipating a showdown—me, defending her from her monstrous father. Forcing him to his knees and grilling him until he confessed, revealed where he'd stashed his decades of loot. The triumphant hero, with the girl on my arm. Devastated yet grateful. Her company salvaged. Her reputation intact. Cue the music and ending credits. Bring down the curtain. Happily-ever-after.

Guess I'm as dumb as the next guy. I never stopped to consider that with her father exposed, Thorne & Company would lose everything. Its prestige. Its hallmark of unparalleled excellence. Its allure. That it will become fodder for months of salacious gossip and envious payback, of splashy front-page news on his spectacular trial, and worldwide declarations of appalled dismay from the exclusive clientele, who'll race to divest themselves of their pieces, decrying the outrage, plummeting the company even further into ruin.

Everything lost. Including Ania's reputation. Her livelihood. Her reason for existing.

When I finally speak, I don't expect the words that come out of my mouth. "Did it for you, huh? I'll bet. He did it for himself. For Virgil Thorne, king shit of the jewelry world."

She lunges at me with an incoherent wail. She's beyond fatigued at this point, beaten to a pulp, but boy, can she pack a wallop. The crack of her hand across my face is like a gunshot, and the punches she aims at my stomach, my chest, anywhere she can, hurt like hell. She might be in need of a hamburger, but in a boxing ring, the girl could hold her own.

I have to fend her off, block her with my arms until she's panting. Only then can I seize her by the wrists and yank her toward me.

She levels her knee and nails me right in the groin.

As I double over, breathless from the agony of it, she suddenly moans. Drops to her knees before me. Covers her face with her hands and starts to cry. No, not cry. Sob. With heartbreaking anguish.

Once I can catch my breath and ensure my parts haven't suffered any permanent damage, I crouch beside her. Wait until she exhausts herself.

"I didn't think it through. I'm sorry, Ania. You have no idea. I didn't know. Didn't—"

Her hand grasps mine. Holds it tightly for a moment. The cool touch of her skin—after her impressive fighting demonstration, how can she not be blazing like a furnace?—strikes me harder and hurts me more than anything she's done.

"It's not your fault," she whispers. "It's mine." She lifts her face to me, gazing through her tangled hair. That mantle of hair I sank my face into in a cheap hotel room in Paris, what now seems a lifetime ago. Though she's still colorless as the bedroom carpet and her eyes are red, circled in dark rings, her voice is steady.

"You're right."

"I am?" I brace myself for another assault.

"He did it for himself. King shit." She staggers to her feet, looks around in near disinterest for one of her ballet flats, which went flying as she launched herself at me. "Virgil Thorne can never love anyone as much as he loves himself," she says. When I frown, she adds, "Something my mother told me."

"Right." I watch her retrieve the ballet flat. Pause to gaze into the closet. Pass a hand as if by instinct across her person, tugging at her pullover, haphazardly tucking her hair behind her ears. Straightening her spine. The Ania Thorne I first met, returning to inhabit the shattered little girl who believed fathers do everything for their daughters.

I feel it's safe enough to ask, "Why did you let him go?"

She glances at me over her shoulder. "Do you have your gun?"

"My gun? No. I—I don't have a license to carry a weapon here. I'm an insurance investigator. In Europe. Not a U.S. sheriff." As I hear my hasty justification, a tepid smile spreads across her lips.

"You came all this way after me and didn't bring your gun? What were you planning to do? Accuse him with harsh language? Or did you think he'd beg for forgiveness and ask us to call the police?"

"Ania—"

Her sudden burst of laughter catches me completely off guard. "Aren't we a pair? No gun. No thief. No father."

"You still have a father," I say.

"Not anymore." Her face turns cold. "What he did to me. What he did to all those other companies. The people whose jewels he stole. The lives he destroyed. That—that poor girl he killed in London. He is *not* my father."

I can't help but think everything is turned upside down. I'm supposed to be the one consoling her. Reassuring her, offering the solutions she needs to get through this. Instead, I'm standing with my mouth agape as she walks back toward me and says, very quietly and firmly, "But we still have a leopard to catch. And that's exactly what we're going to do."

"What?"

"Catch him. Bait the trap within his own game." She looks into my eyes. Though I know this will be a very bad idea, I'm riveted. What I'm seeing isn't the Ania Thorne I met. Not the goddess I took to bed or the icy princess who kicked me out of her Paris apartment.

Here, at last, is Virgil Thorne's daughter.

"You can't be serious," I breathe.

"Oh, I am." She lifts her chin. Doesn't take her cat eyes off me. "The one thing he still thinks he has is this." Her foot comes down on the glove. "The Leopard. He'll vanish. Disappear into legend. The one who got away with it. Except, he won't. Because we know how and why he did it. And now that we know, we can lure him out."

"Lure him? Are you actually suggesting…?"

"Are you with me?" She meets my incredulous stare. "I need to know, Jerome. He's on a plane right now. Off to who knows where. I can guess where he'll go first, but he won't stay for long. He's had all this time to prepare. Years to perfect his new life. You think he's going to hide away in some bolt-hole? He must have known this day might come."

"I'll say. I certainly would have planned for it, if I were him."

"And he did. Down to the very last detail. Just like his heists. Never a mistake."

"But you still think we can get to him? How?"

She leans down to pick up the glove. Slides it over her fingers. It's too big. Floppy. Like an accessory made for a giant.

"With this." Her smile shows a hint of teeth. "Who says leopards can't hunt each other? Let's see who bites first."

The Bait
By C. W. Gortner and M.J. Rose
Coming January 4, 2022

Revenge is a diamond best served cold.

A year after THE STEAL, Ania Throne is determined to take back what the Leopard stole from her. Together with her lover and partner, Jerome, she stages a spectacular heist during the Venetian Carnival, to lure out the treacherous mastermind they unmasked. She's willing to risk it all—until her revenge takes a dangerous twist that could cost her what she loves the most.

Jerome Curtis has given up everything for Ania. She needs his help and he's fallen head over heels for the world's most eligible jewelry designer. But when their daring scheme to catch the thief who escaped turns on them, he's targeted for a crime he never wanted to commit—and he has to find a way out fast.

From a glamorous costume gala to the winter canals of Venice, Ania and Jerome must confront the choices they've made and bait a new trap to catch the Leopard, before the Leopard springs his trap on them. This time, the stakes are personal, but with more than diamonds on the line, can they escape the bait or will it separate them forever?

The second novella in To Catch A Leopard, THE BAIT is a nail-biting romantic caper by bestselling authors C.W. Gortner and M.J. Rose.

Mademoiselle Chanel
By C.W. Gortner
Now available!

A stunning novel of iconic fashion designer Coco Chanel—who revolutionized fashion, built an international empire, and become one of the most influential and controversial figures of the twentieth century.

Born into rural poverty, Gabrielle Chanel and her siblings are sent to orphanage after their mother's death. The sisters nurture Gabrielle's exceptional sewing skills, a talent that will propel her into a life far removed from the drudgery of her childhood.

Transforming herself into Coco—a seamstress and sometime torch singer—the petite brunette burns with an incandescent ambition that draws a wealthy gentleman who will become the love of her life. She immerses herself in his world of money and luxury, discovering a freedom that sparks her creativity. But it is only when her lover takes her to Paris that Coco discovers her destiny.

Rejecting the frilly, corseted silhouette of the past, her sleek, minimalist styles reflect the youthful ease and confidence of the 1920s modern woman. As Coco's reputation spreads, her couturier business explodes, taking her into rarefied society circles and bohemian salons. But her fame and fortune cannot save her from heartbreak as the years pass. And when Paris falls to the Nazis, she is forced to make choices that will haunt her.

Mademoiselle Chanel explores the inner world of a woman of staggering ambition whose strength, passion and artistic vision would become her trademark.

The Last Tiara
By M.J. Rose
Now Available

A provocative and moving story of a young female architect in post-World War II Manhattan who stumbles upon a hidden treasure and begins a journey to discovering her mother's life during the fall of the Romanovs.

Sophia Moon had always been reticent about her life in Russia and when she dies, suspiciously, on a wintry New York evening, Isobelle despairs that her mother's secrets have died with her. But while renovating the apartment they shared, Isobelle discovers something among her mother's effects — a stunning silver tiara, stripped of its jewels.

Isobelle's research into the tiara's provenance draws her closer to her mother's past — including the story of what became of her father back in Russia, a man she has never known. The facts elude her until she meets a young jeweler who wants to help her but is conflicted by his loyalty to the Midas Society, a covert international organization whose mission is to return lost and stolen antiques, jewels, and artwork to their original owners.

Told in alternating points of view, the stories of the two young women unfurl as each struggles to find their way during two separate wars. In 1915, young Sofiya Petrovitch, favorite of the royal household and best friend of Grand Duchess Olga Nikolaevna, tends to wounded soldiers in a makeshift hospital within the grounds of the Winter Palace in St. Petersburg and finds the love of her life. In 1948 New York, Isobelle Moon works to break through the rampant sexism of the age as one of very few women working in a male-dominated profession and discovers far more about love and family than she ever hoped for.

In the two narratives, the secrets of Sofiya's early life are revealed incrementally, even as Isobelle herself works to solve the mystery of the historic Romanov tiara (which is based on an actual Romanov artifact that is, to this day, still missing) and how it is that her mother came to possess it. The two strands play off each other in finely-tuned counterpoint, building to a series of surprising and deeply satisfying revelations.

About C. W. Gortner

C.W. GORTNER holds an MFA in Writing with an emphasis in Renaissance Studies from the New College of California, as well as an AA from the Fashion Institute of Design and Merchandising in San Francisco.

After an eleven year-long career in fashion, during which he worked as a vintage retail buyer, freelance publicist, and fashion show coordinator, C.W. devoted the next twelve years to the public health sector. In 2012, he became a full-time writer following the international success of his novels.

In his extensive travels to research his books, he has danced a galliard at Hampton Court, learned about organic gardening at Chenoceaux, and spent a chilly night in a ruined Spanish castle. His books have garnered widespread acclaim and been translated into twenty-one languages to date, with over 400,000 copies sold. A sought-after public speaker. C.W. has given keynote addresses at writer conferences in the US and abroad. He is also a dedicated advocate for animal rights, in particular companion animal rescue to reduce shelter overcrowding.

C.W. recently completed his fourth novel for Ballantine Books, about Lucrezia Borgia; the third novel in his Tudor Spymaster series for St Martin's Press; and a new novel about the dramatic, glamorous life of Coco Chanel, scheduled for lead title publication by William Morrow, Harper Collins, in the spring of 2015.

Half-Spanish by birth and raised in southern Spain, C.W. now lives in Northern California with his partner and two very spoiled rescue cats.

To find out more about his work, visit: http://www.cwgortner.com

About M.J. Rose

New York Times bestseller M.J. Rose grew up in New York City mostly in the labyrinthine galleries of the Metropolitan Museum, the dark tunnels and lush gardens of Central Park and reading her mother's favorite books before she was allowed. She believes mystery and magic are all around us but we are too often too busy to notice... books that exaggerate mystery and magic draw attention to it and remind us to look for it and revel in it.

Please visit her blog, Museum of Mysteries at http://www.mjrose.com/blog/

Rose's work has appeared in many magazines including *Oprah* magazine and she has been featured in the *New York Times, Newsweek, Wall Street Journal, Time, USA Today* and on the Today Show, and NPR radio. Rose graduated from Syracuse University, spent the '80s in advertising, has a commercial in the Museum of Modern Art in New York City and since 2005 has run the first marketing company for authors - Authorbuzz.com.

Rose lives in Connecticut with her husband, the musician and composer Doug Scofield.